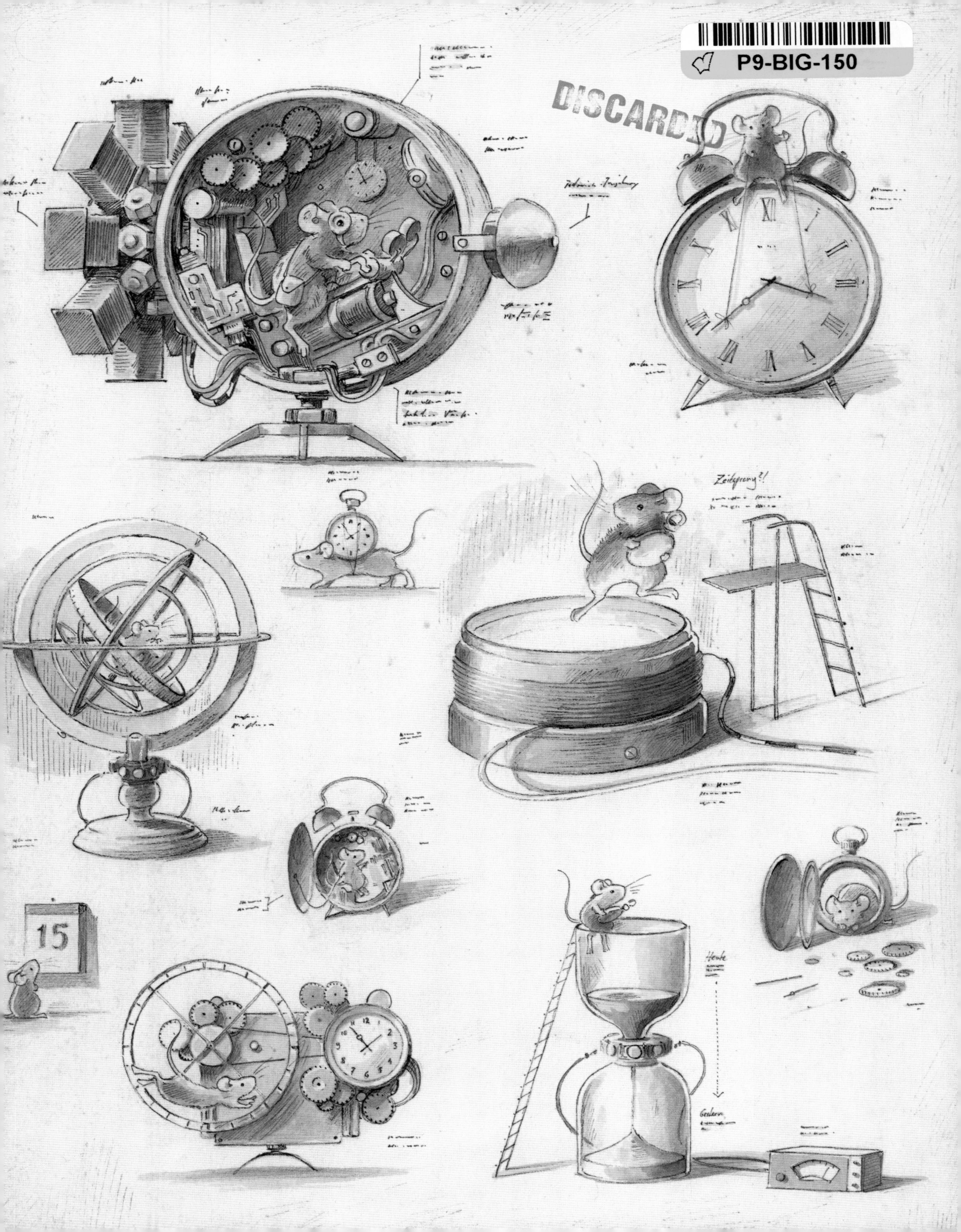
Zeitsprung?!
15
Heute
Gestern

"Whoever spends too much time trying to master time
will find that in time . . . time will master him."
—*Old mousy proverb*

EINSTEIN

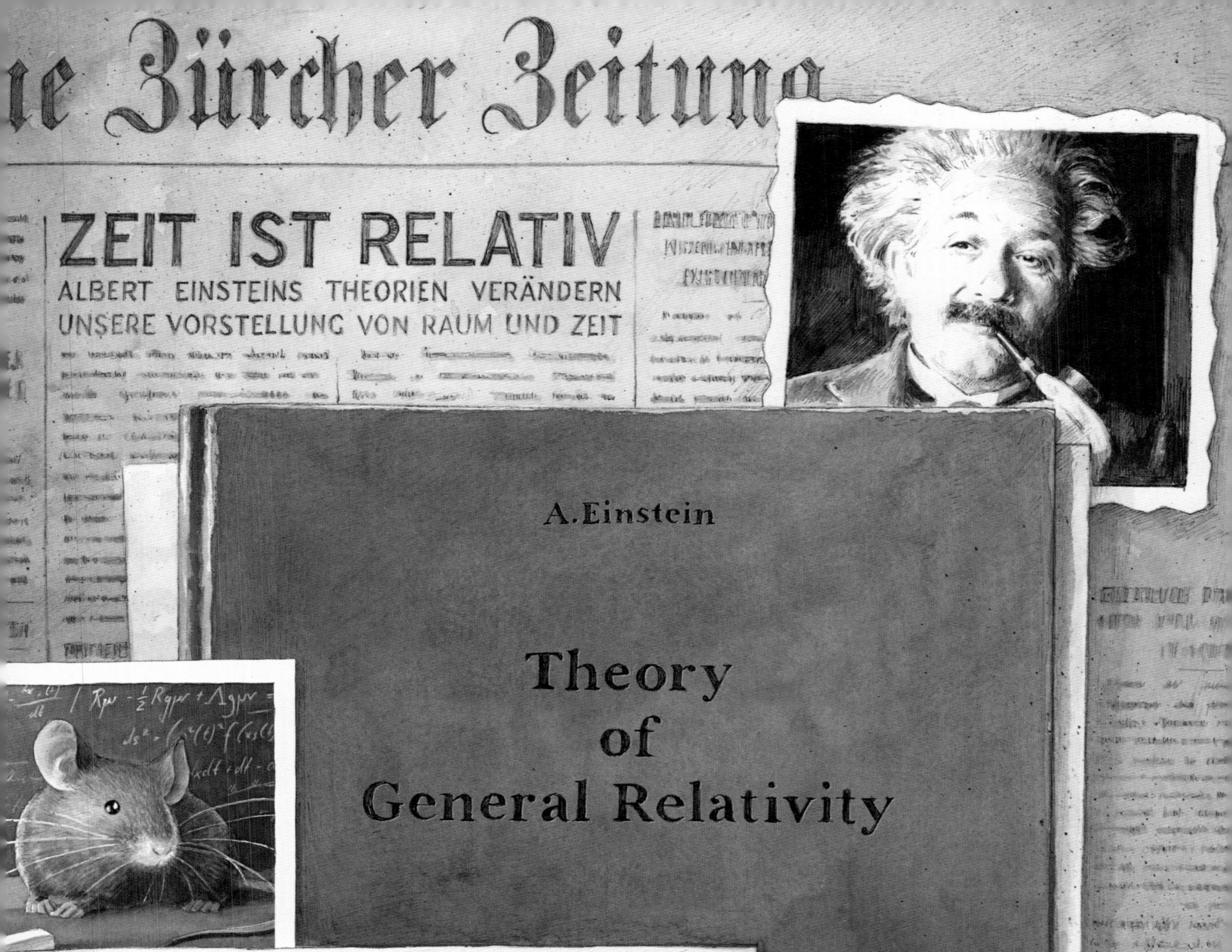
e Zürcher Zeitung
ZEIT IST RELATIV
ALBERT EINSTEINS THEORIEN VERÄNDERN
UNSERE VORSTELLUNG VON RAUM UND ZEIT
A. Einstein
Theory of General Relativity

First published in Switzerland in 2020 by NordSüd Verlag under the title *Einstein—Die fantastische Reise einer Maus durch Raum und Zeit.*

Translated by David Henry Wilson
Book design by Torben Kuhlmann
First published in the United States, Great Britain, Canada, Australia, and New Zealand in 2021 by NorthSouth Books, Inc., an imprint of NordSüd Verlag AG, CH-8050 Zürich, Switzerland.

Distributed in the United States by NorthSouth Books Inc., New York 10016.
Library of Congress Cataloging-in-Publication Data is available.
ISBN: 978-0-7358-4444-5 (trade edition)
Printed in Latvia
1 3 5 7 9 • 10 8 6 4 2
www.northsouth.com

Torben Kuhlmann

EINSTEIN

The Fantastic Journey of a Mouse Through Space and Time

Translated by David Henry Wilson

North
South

Waiting

Three hands wandered over the dial of the mouse's pocket watch. The small cog-wheels inside the brass casing produced a soft and regular tick-tock. The thinnest of the three hands moved fastest and was just about to start another round.

The term "pocket watch" wasn't quite right from a mouse's perspective. The watch was bigger than he, and so it would never have fitted into his pocket. The little mouse counted the last few seconds until all the hands stood together on twelve. In the distance, bells rang out to announce midnight and the beginning of a new day. This was the moment the mouse had been waiting for. He ran into the next room, where there was a calendar hanging on the wall. A human calendar. Every night he would tear off another sheet, which wasn't easy for a mouse. He had to use his whole body and all his strength in order to tear the paper. But every sheet he removed brought him closer to this very day, and with each passing hour he became more and more excited.

Thursday
5

Friday
6

Saturday
7

Sunday
8

Monday
9

10

Tuesday
10

Wednesday
11

Thursday
12

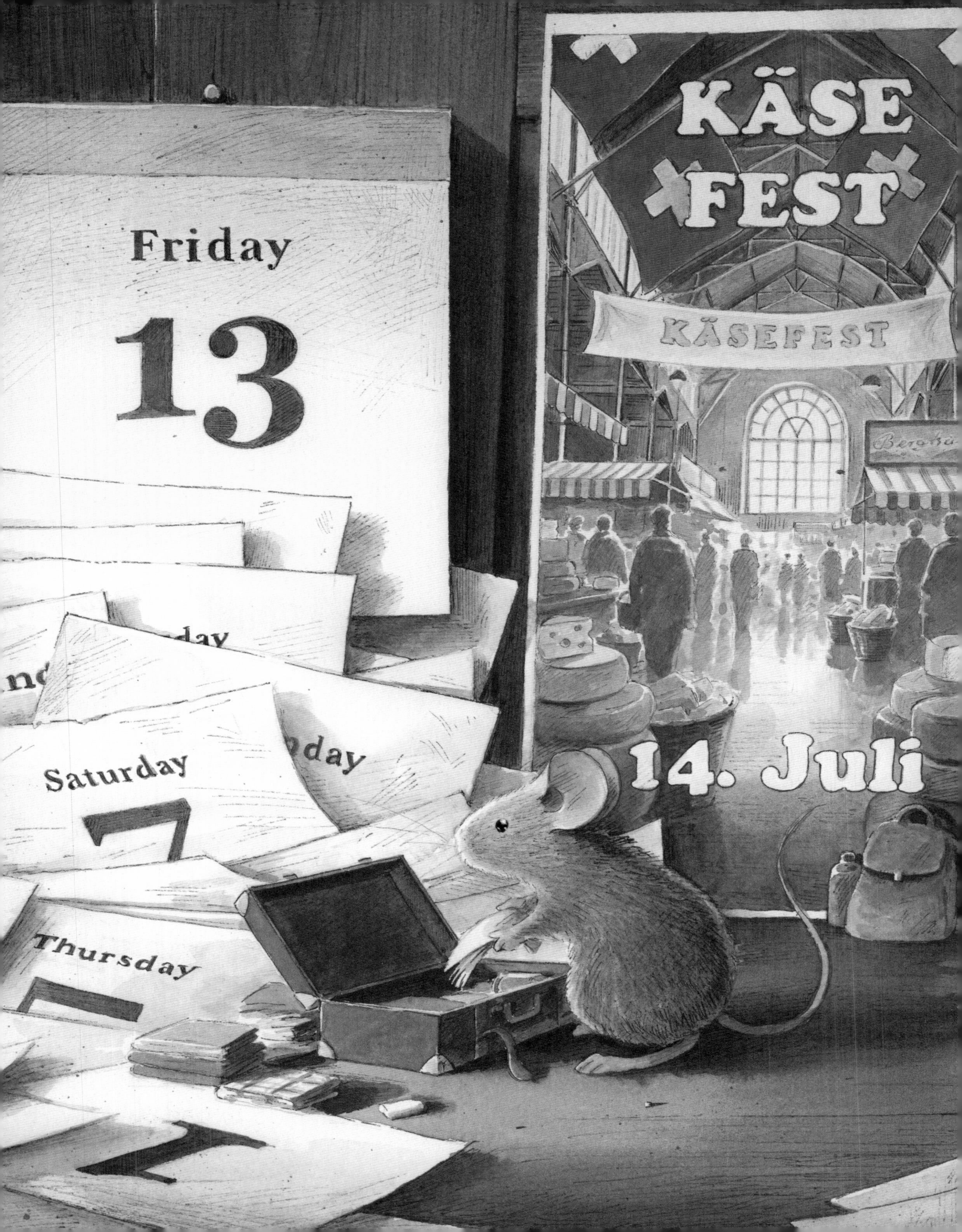
Friday
13
KÄSE
FEST
KÄSEFEST
Saturday
7
Thursday
14. Juli

Every mouse's dream

The long wait was over—the fair of fairs was about to start. Some time ago the mouse had heard humans talking about it. "The biggest cheese fair the world has ever seen," said one of them. "The finest cheese specialties from every nation," said another, who sounded rather professorial. The mouse had stolen a small brochure from the professor's briefcase when he wasn't looking. Camembert, Brie, Gouda, Emmentaler, Cheddar, Pecorino. The mouse's whiskers trembled with excitement at the very thought of all that cheese. And this was the day when at last he would set off to the great cheese fair. . . .

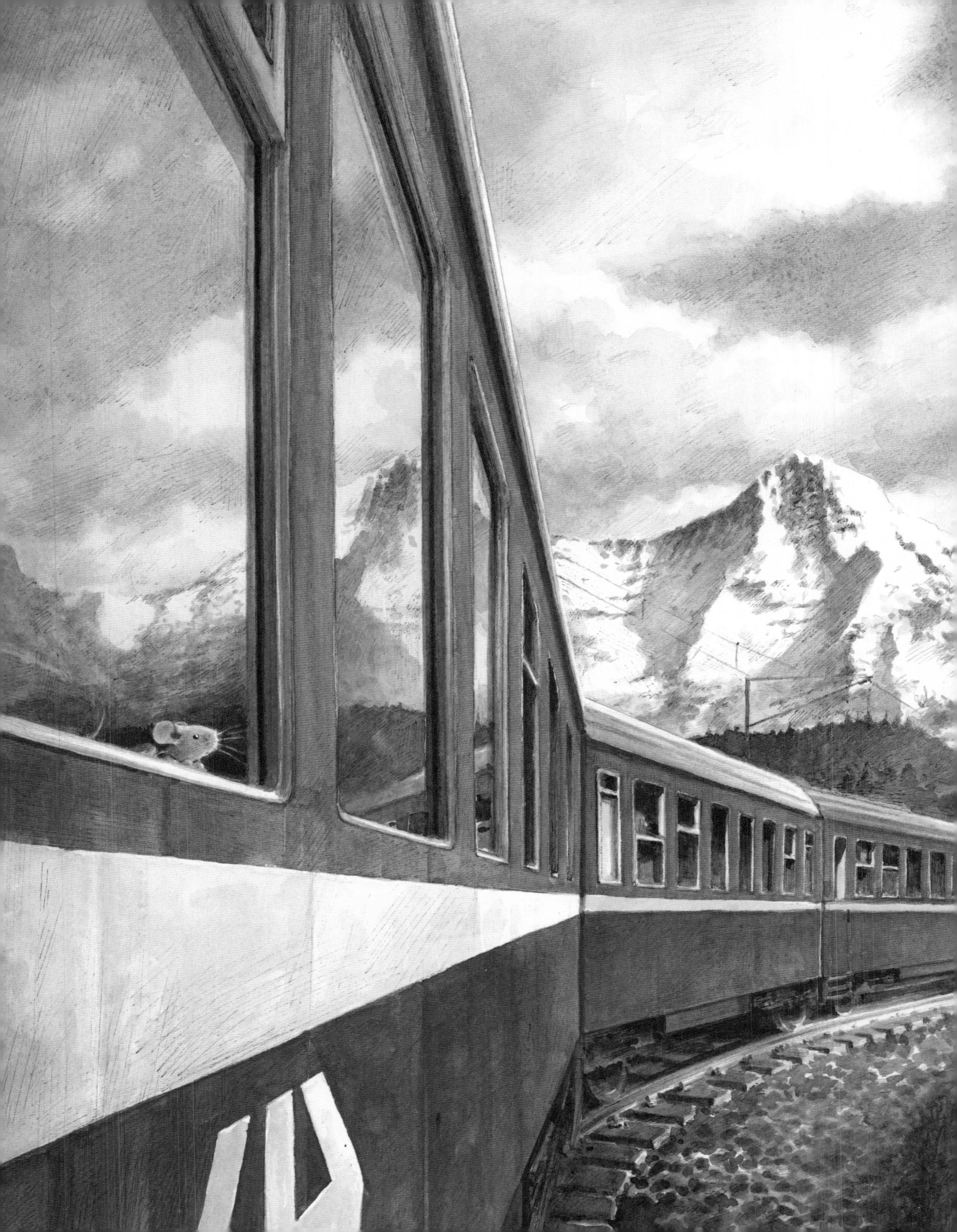

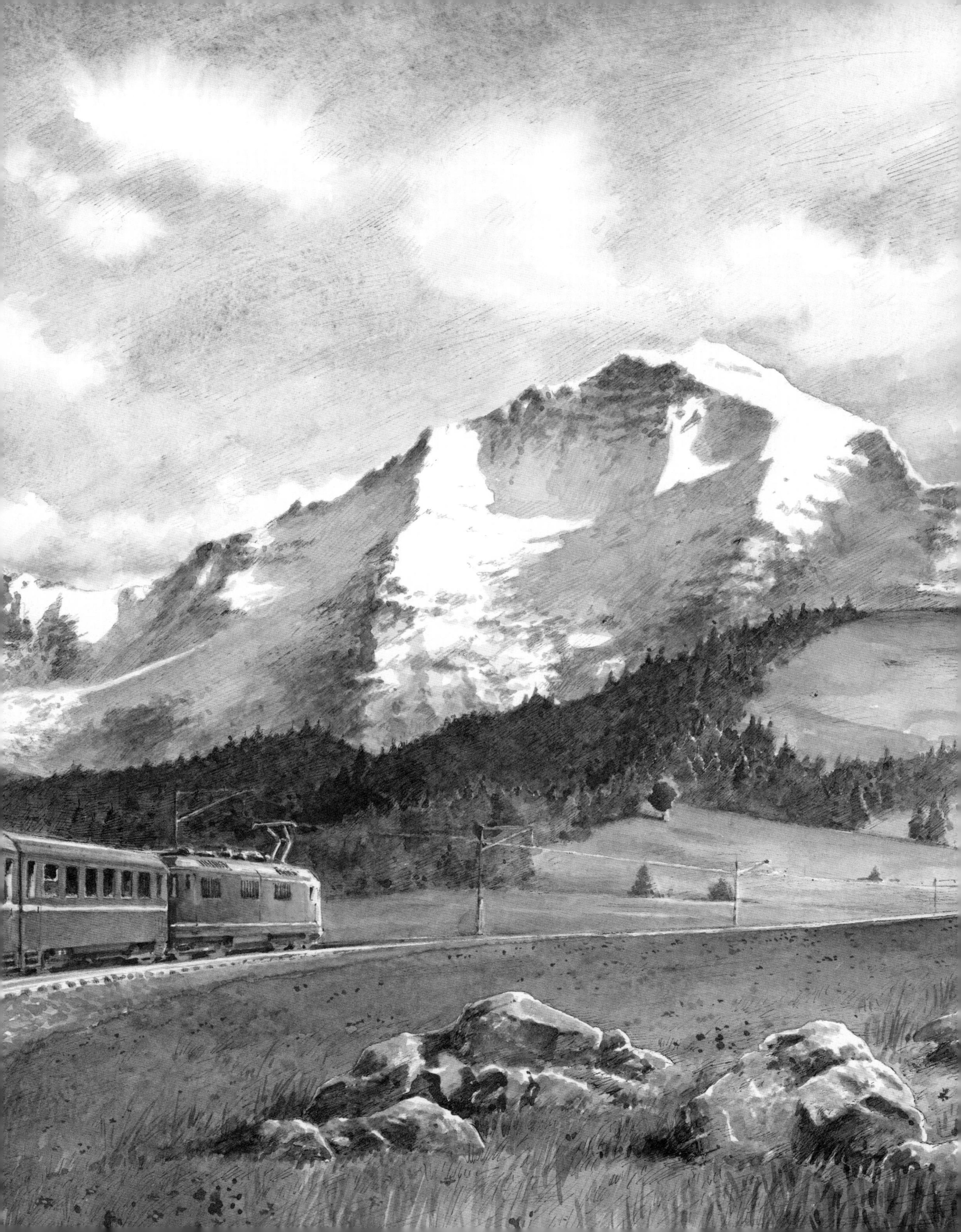

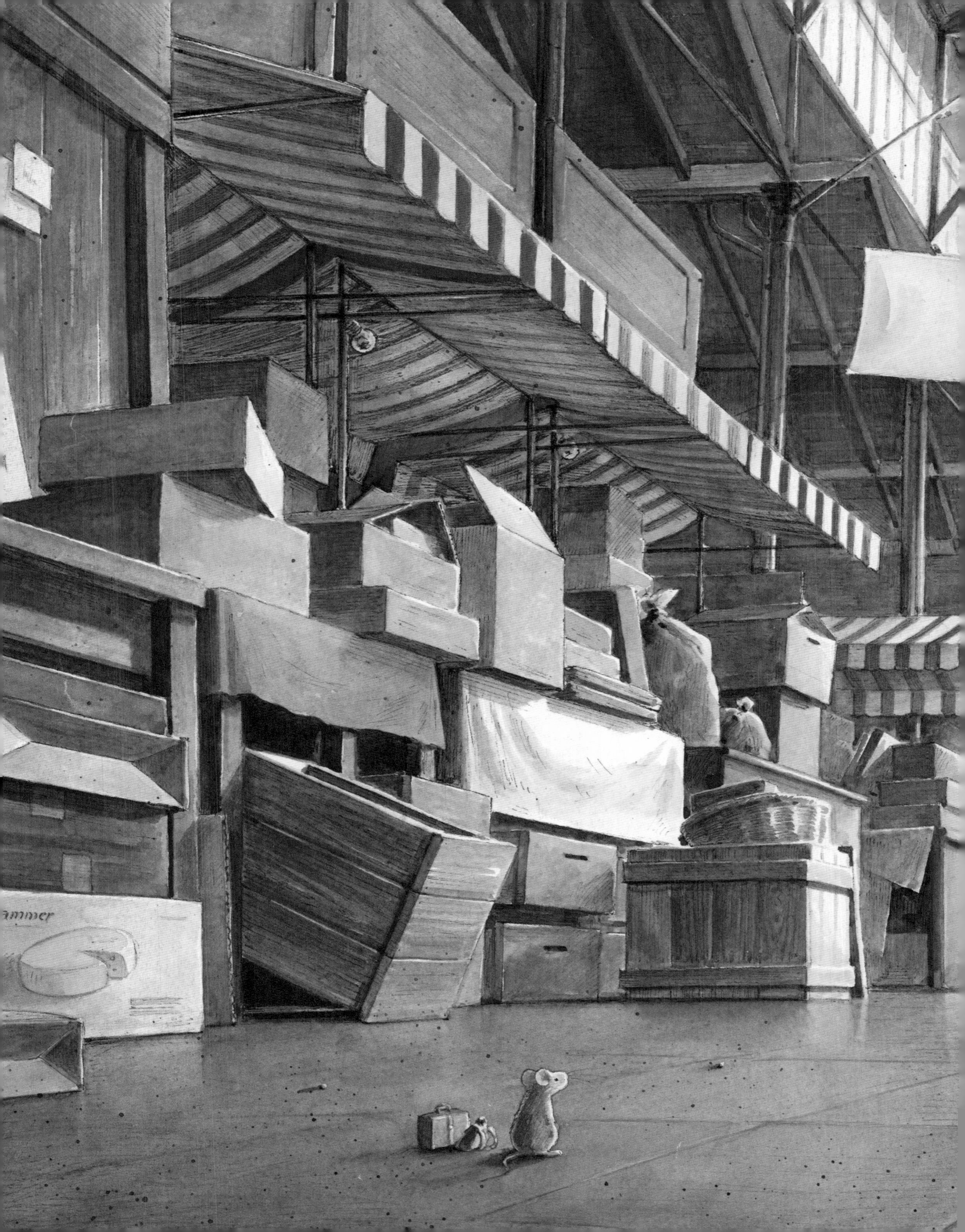
ammer

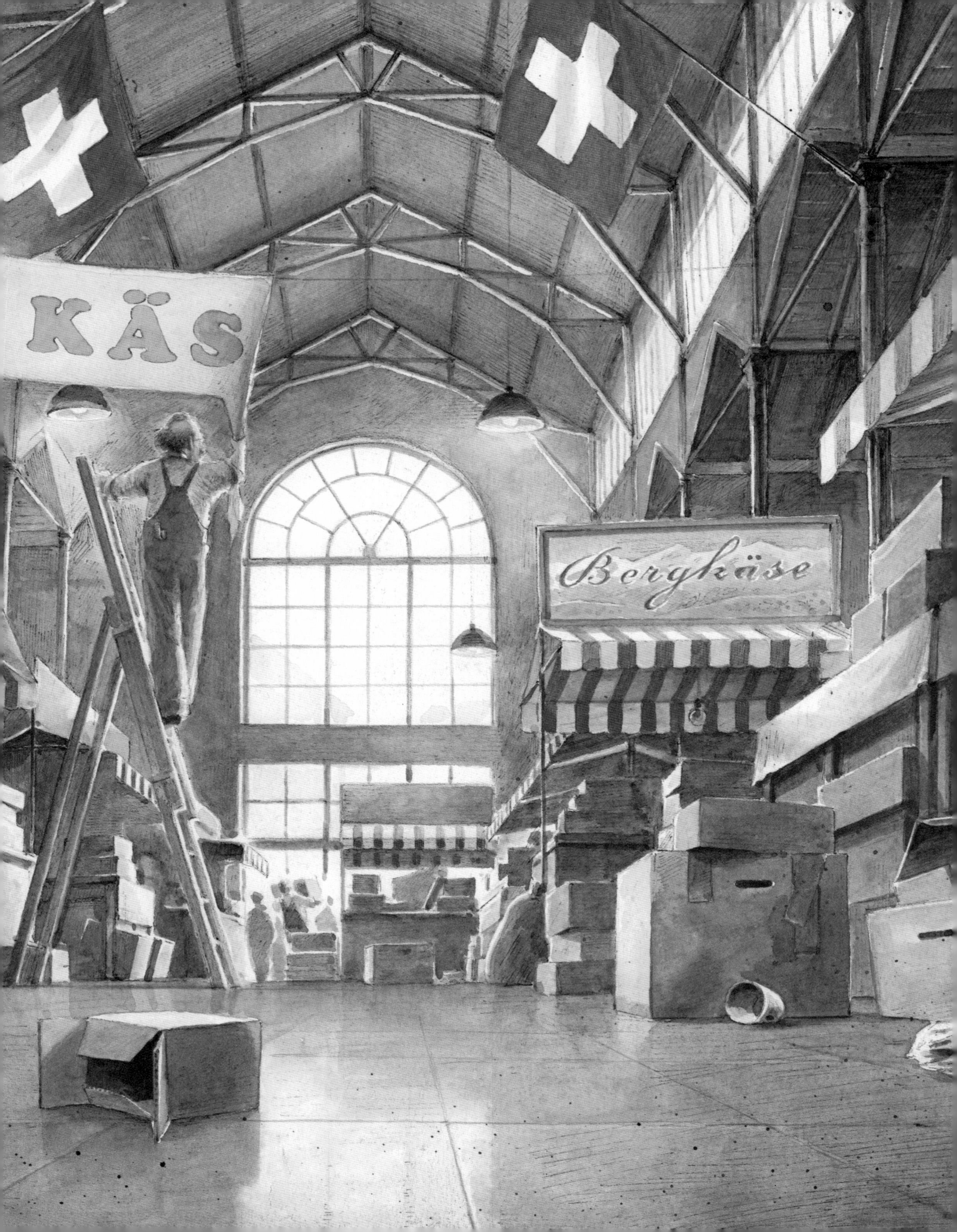
KÄS
Bergkäse

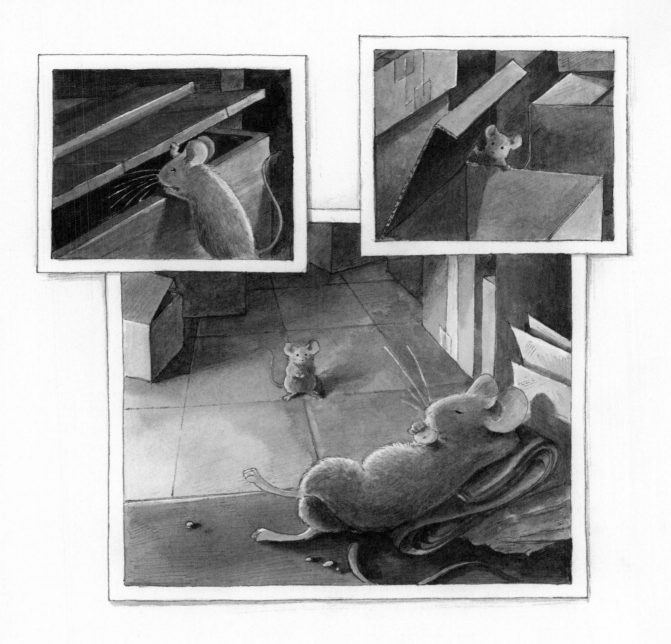

What had happened? No sign of cheese anywhere! Just a few workmen in overalls carrying boxes around. What did it all mean?

The mouse hunted everywhere. Surely there must be a bit of cheese lying around somewhere. But all the cartons and boxes were empty. Then from somewhere an unmistakable scent came wafting into his nostrils.

A rather plump mouse with a very full stomach was lying on top of a wooden crate happily nibbling away at a piece of cheese. It was a piece of spicy hard cheese. Maybe from the Swiss Alps?

"Excuse me," said the little mouse rather shyly. "Please can you tell me where I can find the great cheese fair?"

"Cheese fair?" said the munching mouse as he deftly flicked the last piece of cheese into his mouth. He spoke with a Swiss accent. "That was yesterday, Einstein!" The last word sounded sarcastic. The mouse smacked his lips and licked his fingertips. "You're a day late!"

"But I've come a long way for this!" protested the little mouse. Even as he said it, he realized that it wouldn't change anything.

"Well, you'll just have to turn back time, won't you?" said the portly mouse with a giggle and a sneer, and after licking up one last crumb of cheese got up to go.

The little mouse was all alone in the great exhibition hall.

"Too late . . . a whole day too late . . . How could that have happened?" the little mouse kept asking himself. He had counted the days so carefully, and every night he'd torn just one sheet off the calendar. He racked his brain. Had he miscounted? Had he forgotten a day? Or had he gone to sleep before midnight without tearing off a sheet?

Who fiddled with the watch?

In the meantime, the sun had disappeared behind the mountains and night lay over the town. Lost in thought, the little mouse wandered through the alleyways; the words of the plump mouse kept running through his head. How could one turn time backward? He'd said it in a way that sounded like a joke, but why shouldn't it be possible to reverse time? The mouse plodded on through the darkness, his mind racing. And what was the point of the funny name the other mouse had called him? Einstein? "That isn't my name!" he murmured to himself.

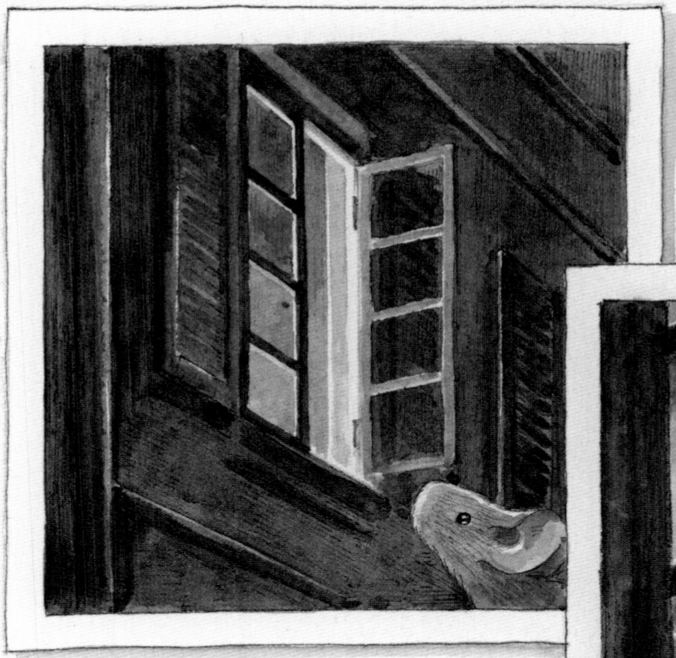

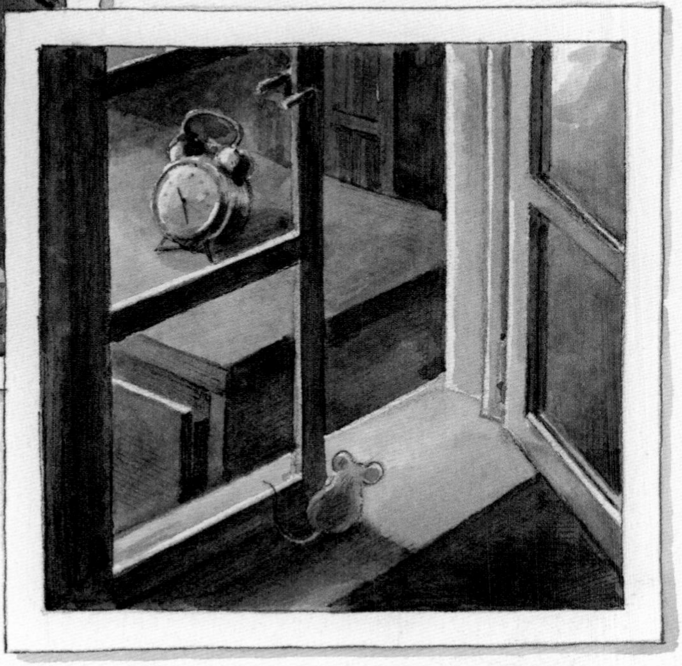

Suddenly a familiar sound came out through an open window. It was the rhythmic ticking of a clock. The mouse climbed up the rusty drainpipe and sat down on the windowsill. On a dressing table not far from the window stood an alarm clock. The hands circled round the dial, just as they did on his pocket watch. He gazed at it for a while, then boldly hopped into the room, grabbed hold of the hand that marked the seconds, and held it tight.

"According to this clock, time can stand still!" he whispered to himself, and looked around expectantly. The dark room seemed unchanged. Nothing moved. There was no sound. Was time really standing still? Next the mouse gripped the minute hand and used all his strength to turn it back in the opposite direction.

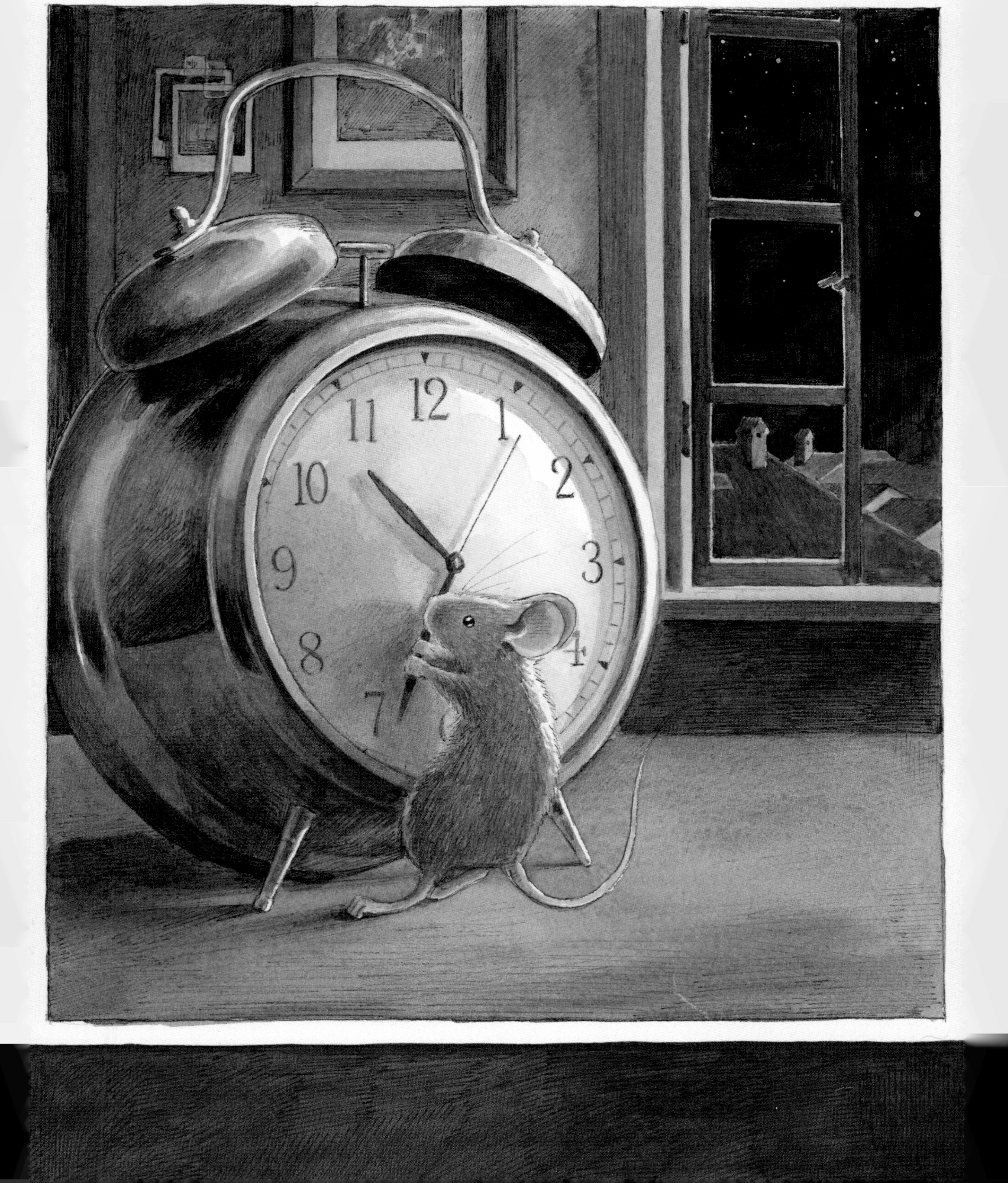

Once again he could not detect any change. He had turned the minute hand backward around the dial ten or eleven times, and the hour hand actually moved in the same direction as the minute hand—backward around the dial. Now the alarm clock displayed a time that ought to have been early in the afternoon. But outside it was still dark night.

"So that's not how it works." He had turned the clock back. But not time itself.

Then once again he heard something. With his sensitive ears he picked up another ticking from the room next door. He went out into the corridor, and from there he could see a huge grandfather clock in the living room. There was also a bedroom door that was slightly ajar, and through that came the sound of someone snoring and the pale light of a radio alarm. Instead of hands, lit digits told the time. And wasn't that a wristwatch lying on the bedside table?

The little mouse's brain was working hard. "Maybe I have to turn several clocks back at the same time? . . ."

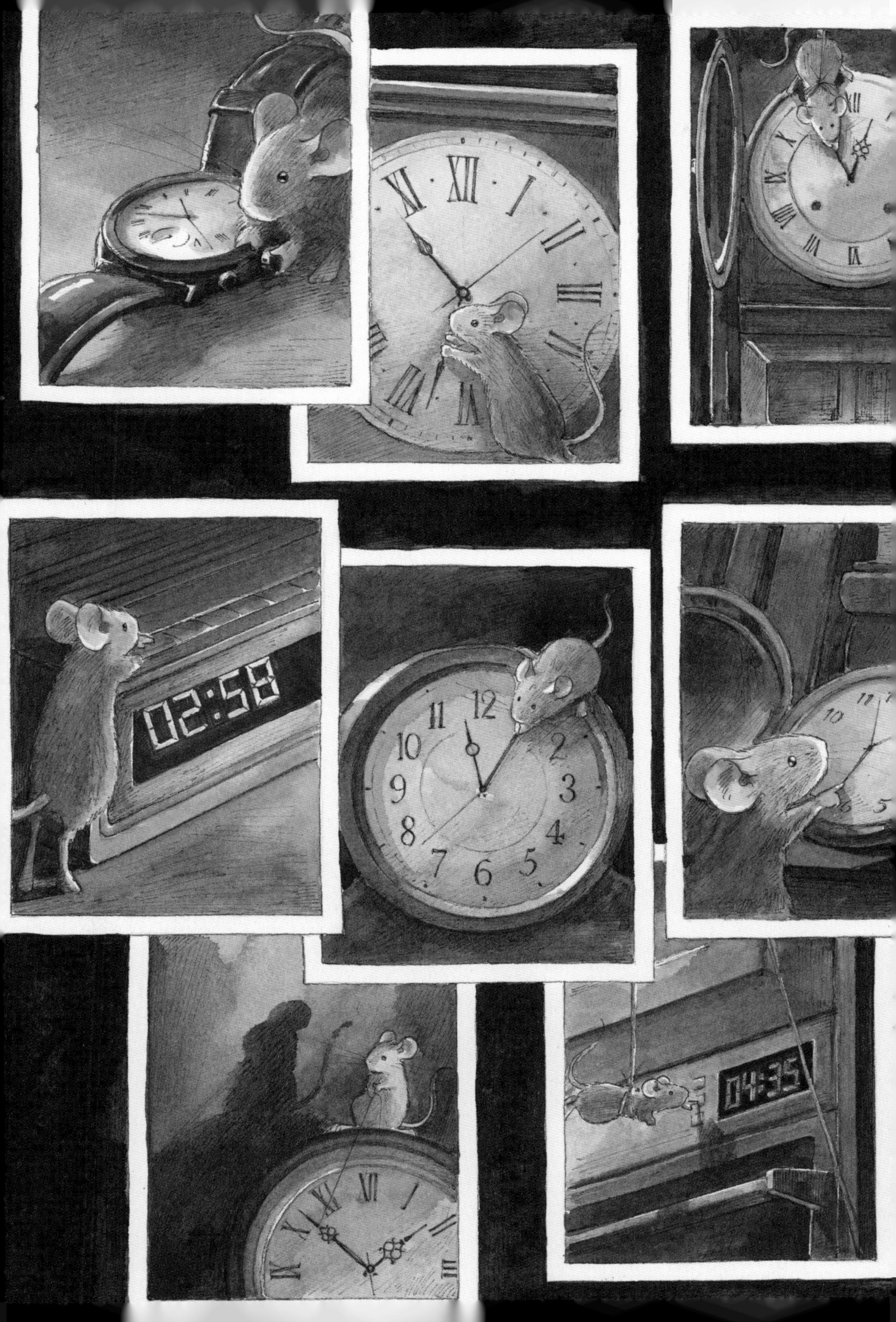
02:58
04:35

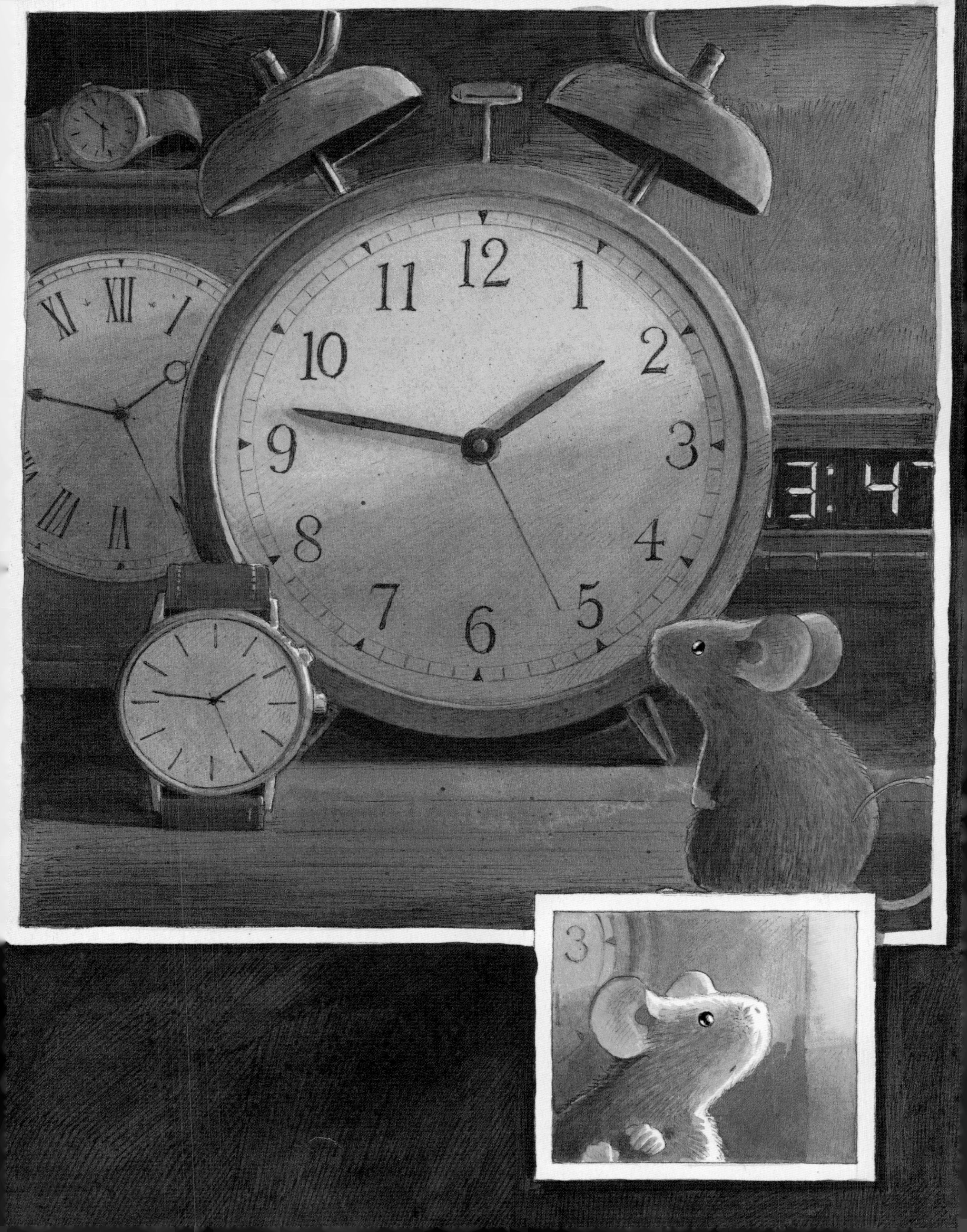

The little mouse was exhausted. With a great effort he had found every clock and watch in the house and turned each one back to early afternoon. But instead of reliving yesterday afternoon, he could see that despite all the reversing of all the clocks, the morning sun was now rising over the rooftops in the east. And the dark apartment was gradually being filled with a warm yellow light.

"Experiment failed," confessed the little mouse, and again his face lapsed into thoughtfulness. "It makes no difference how many clocks I turn back; time still goes forward."

A loud noise suddenly jerked him out of his thoughts. Somewhere in the neighborhood the bell from a clock tower had begun to chime the hour. Was this a sign? At that moment the mouse knew what he now had to do. Once and for all he must find out whether clocks influenced the flow of time. . . .

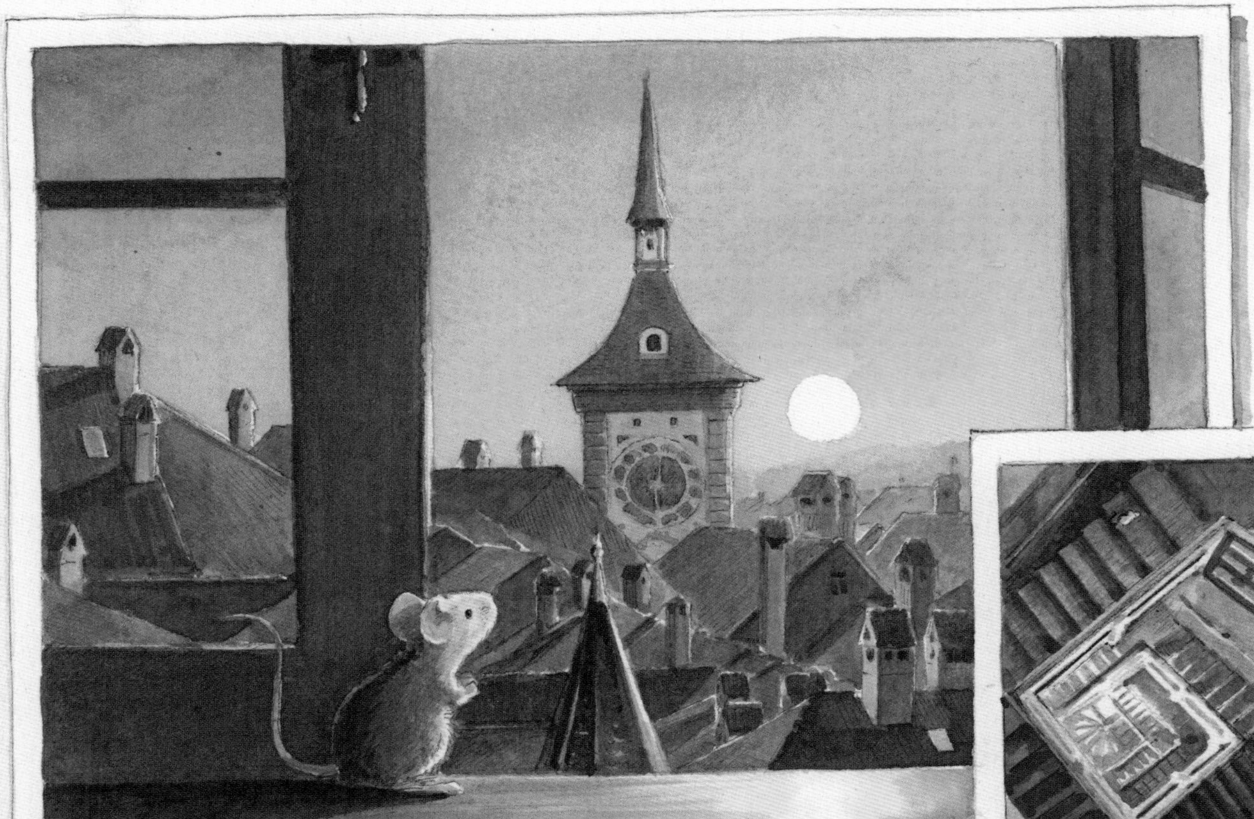

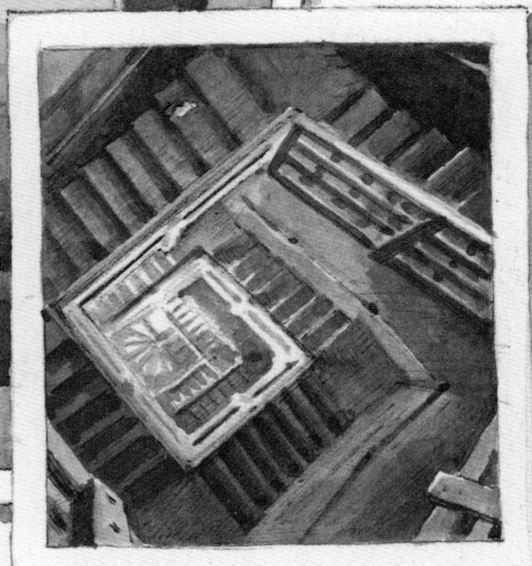

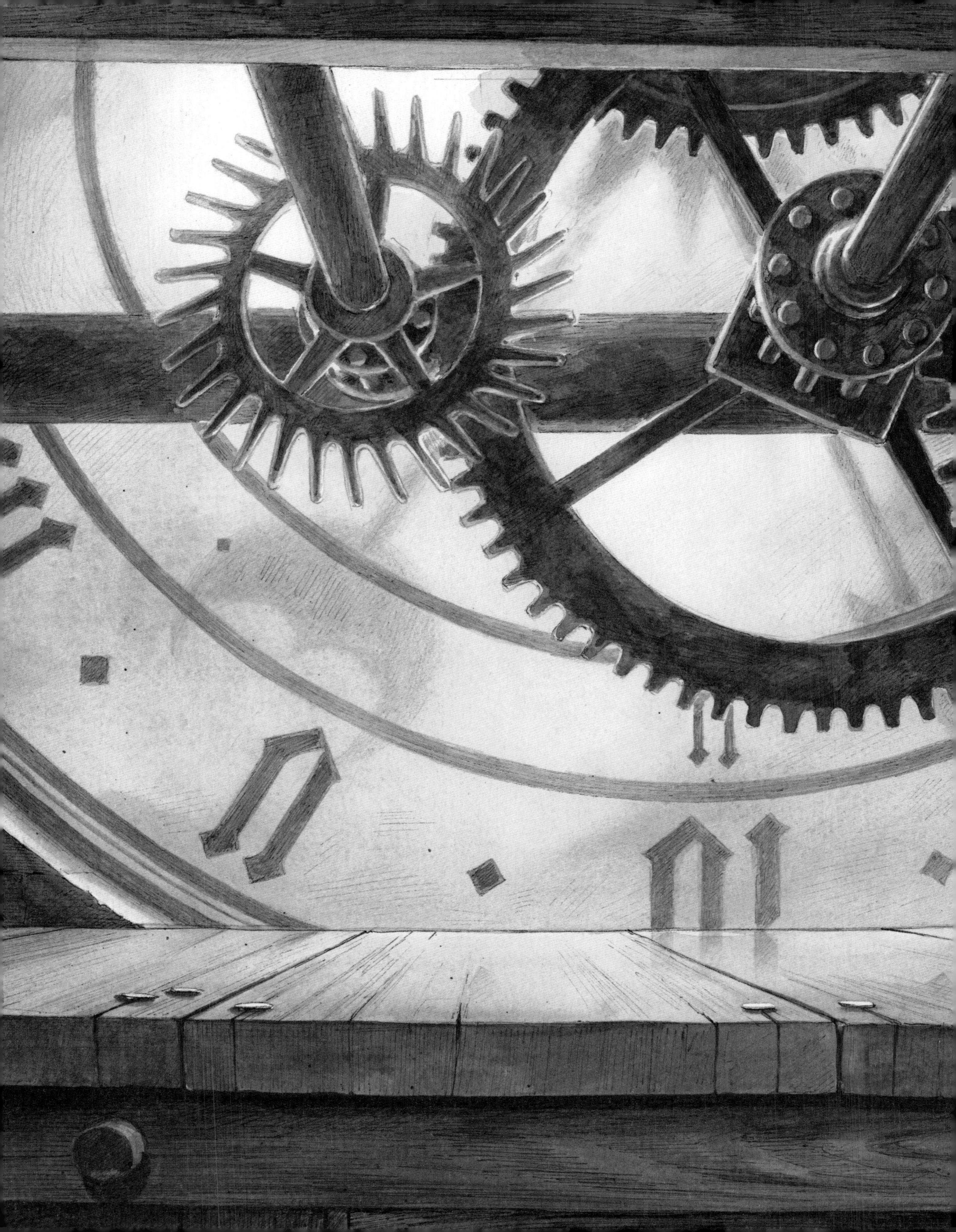

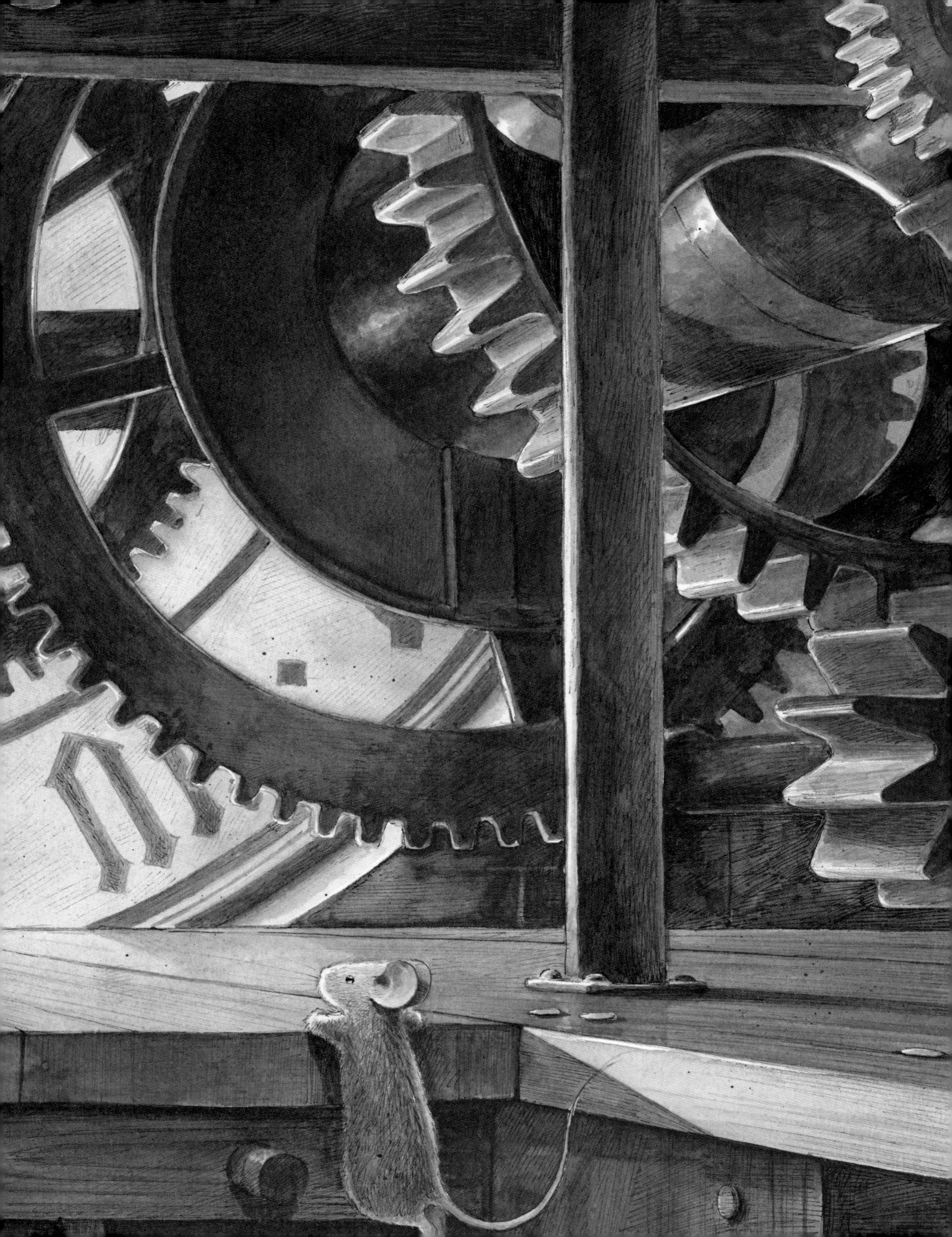

The biggest clock in town

The clock tower was several stories high and had beautifully decorated faces. The mouse climbed up the spiral staircase that led to the clock room. He stopped for a moment. It had been hard work climbing all this way, especially for a small mouse. Once he'd got his breath back he turned his attention to the gigantic mechanism. The teeth of the wheels fitted into one another so that one wheel drove the next bigger wheel, and thick iron rods carried the movement over to the hands of the clock outside. The mouse stood awestruck in the midst of this rattling, grinding structure. Then, with a determined look on his face, he picked up a large, rusty screw. . . .

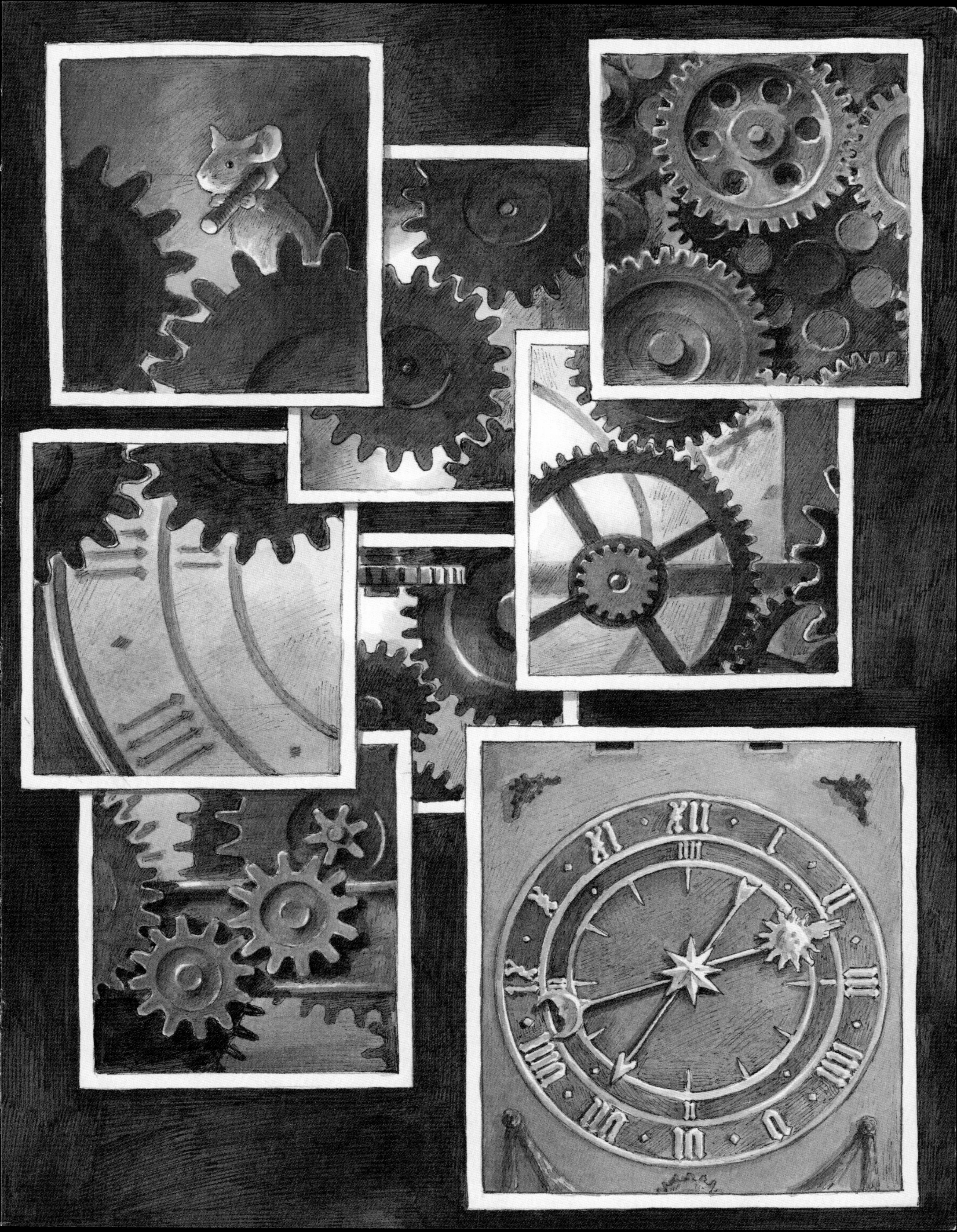

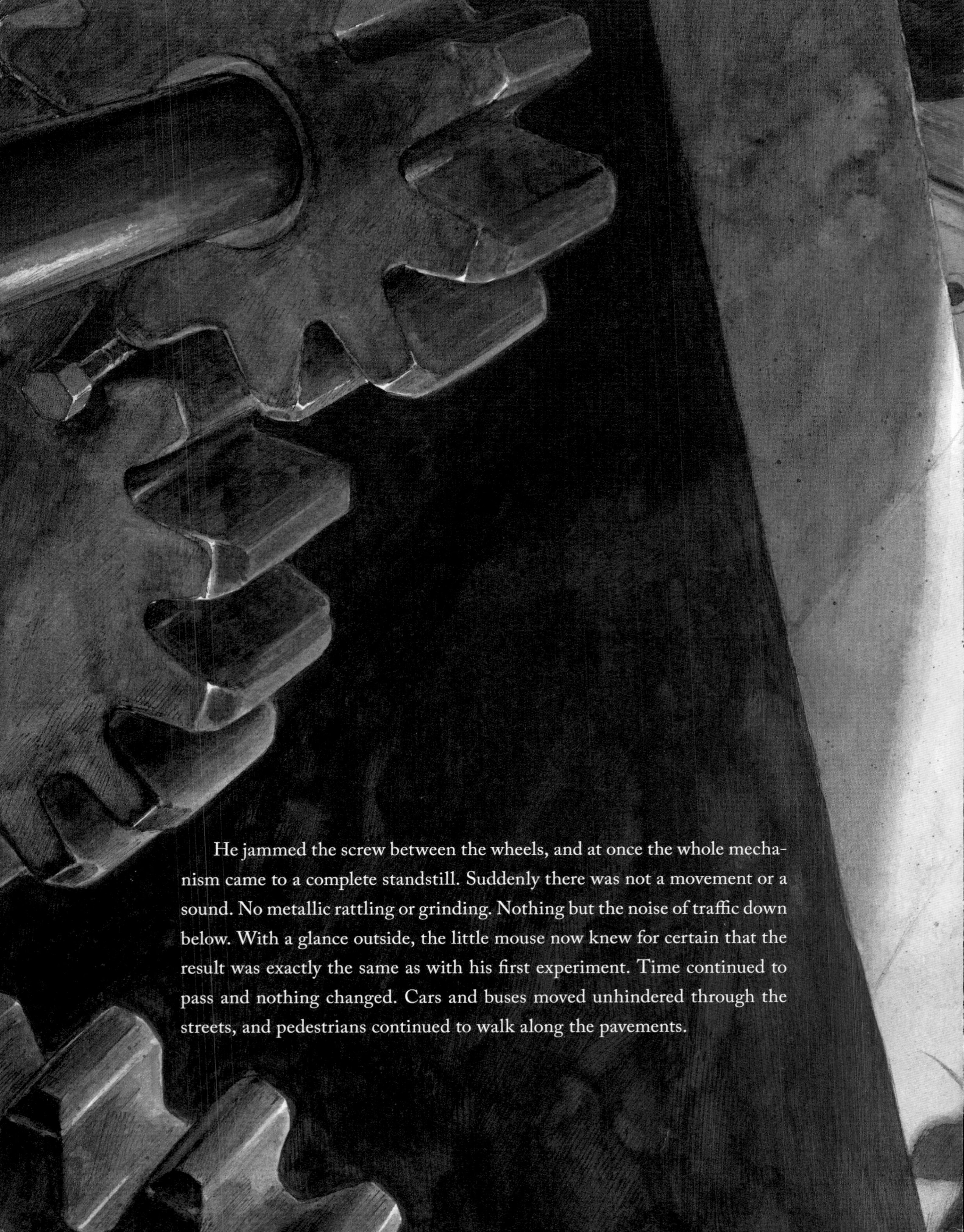

He jammed the screw between the wheels, and at once the whole mechanism came to a complete standstill. Suddenly there was not a movement or a sound. No metallic rattling or grinding. Nothing but the noise of traffic down below. With a glance outside, the little mouse now knew for certain that the result was exactly the same as with his first experiment. Time continued to pass and nothing changed. Cars and buses moved unhindered through the streets, and pedestrians continued to walk along the pavements.

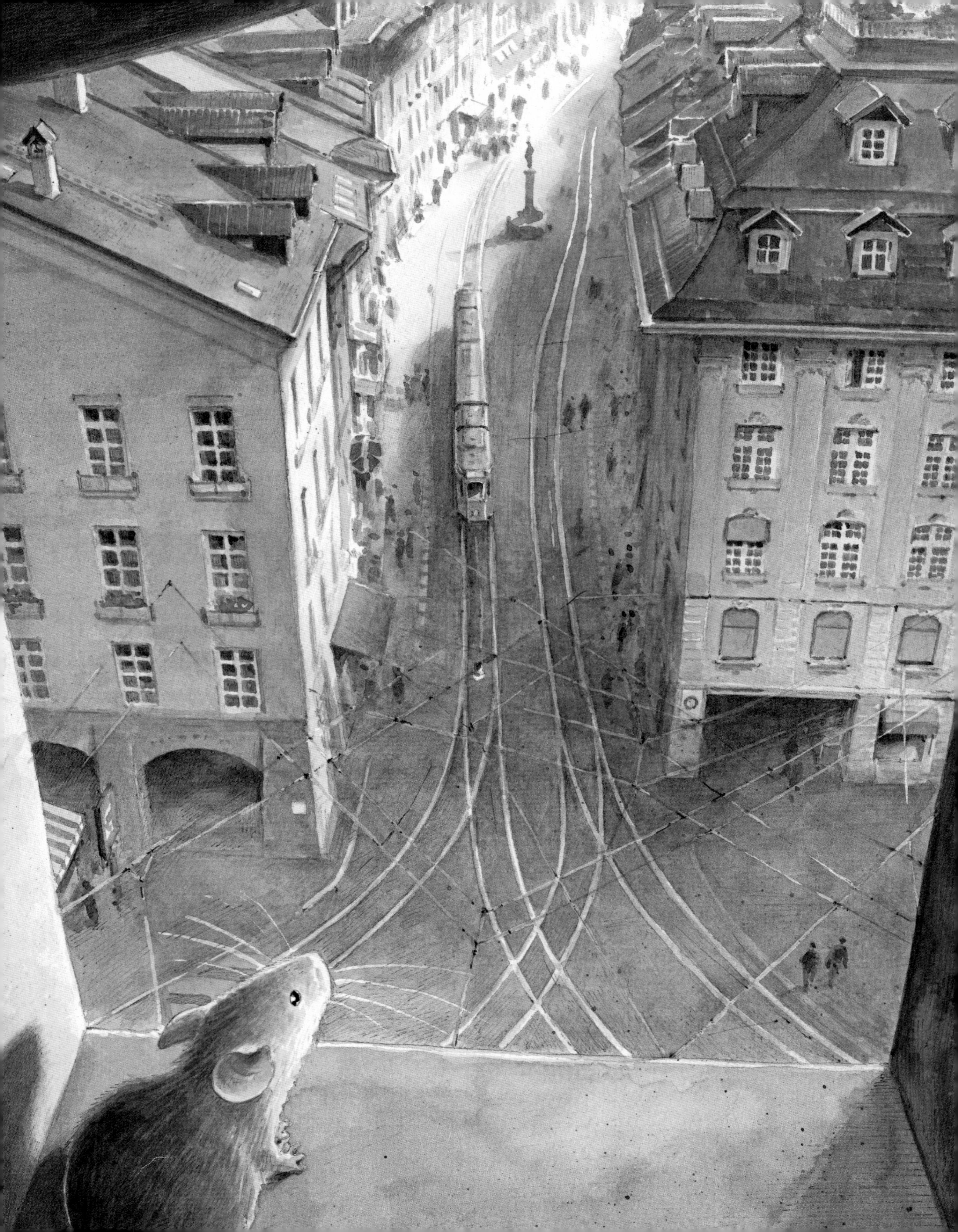

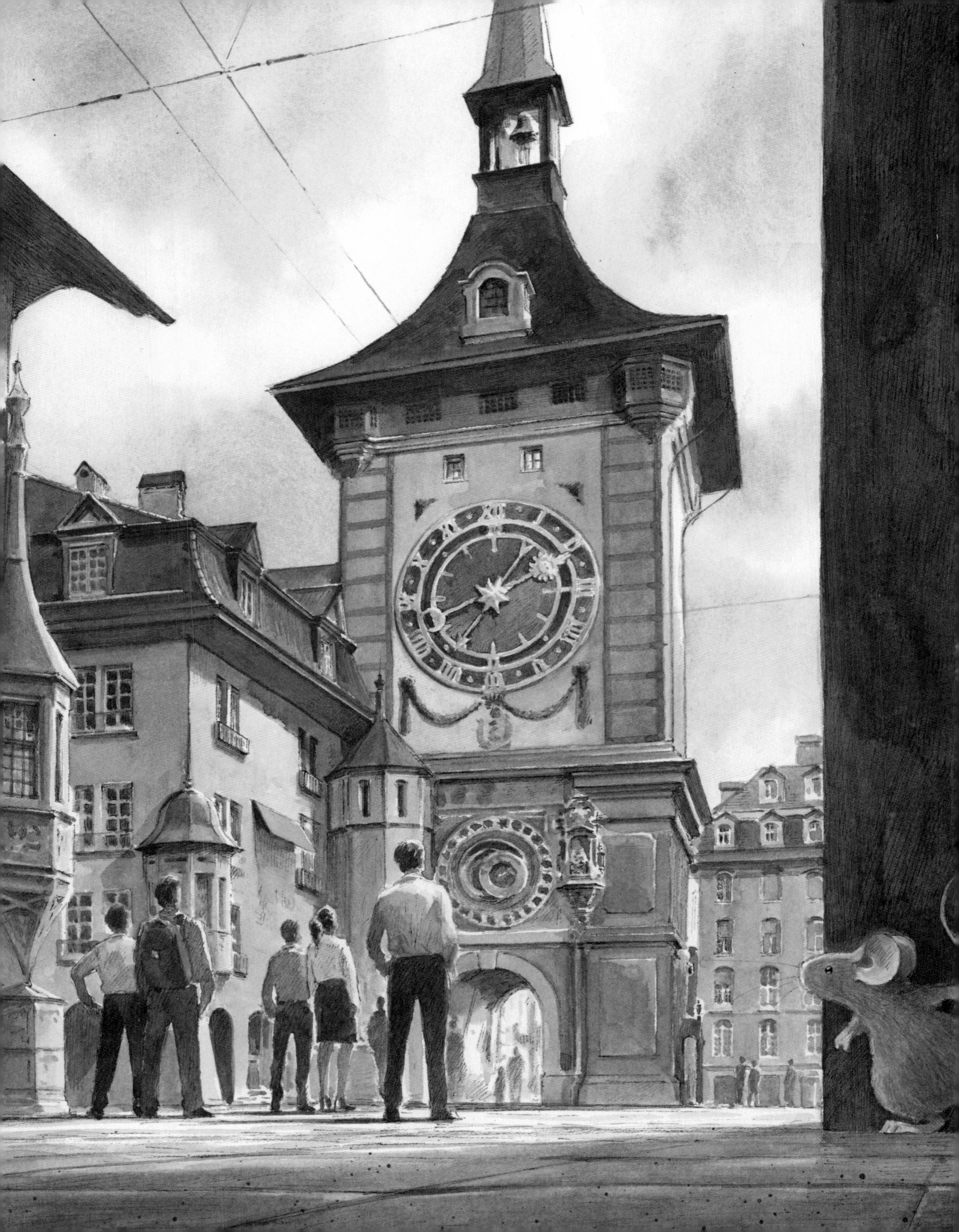

In due course more and more passersby realized that the clock had stopped. They looked at the tower, then at their wristwatches, and then at the tower again. The little mouse saw all this from his safe hiding place. But when a few grim-faced workmen with toolboxes arrived and climbed up the inside of the tower, he scurried away feeling a little ashamed of himself.

"Oh dear, now I've started something," he sighed as he left.

For a few hours he wandered aimlessly through the town, still trying to figure out what time might be and what clocks had to do with it. He was so lost in his thoughts that he almost walked under the shoe of a pedestrian. Only at the very last moment did the man step sideways. Then when he'd recovered from the shock, the little mouse saw a place where perhaps he would find the answers to all his questions.

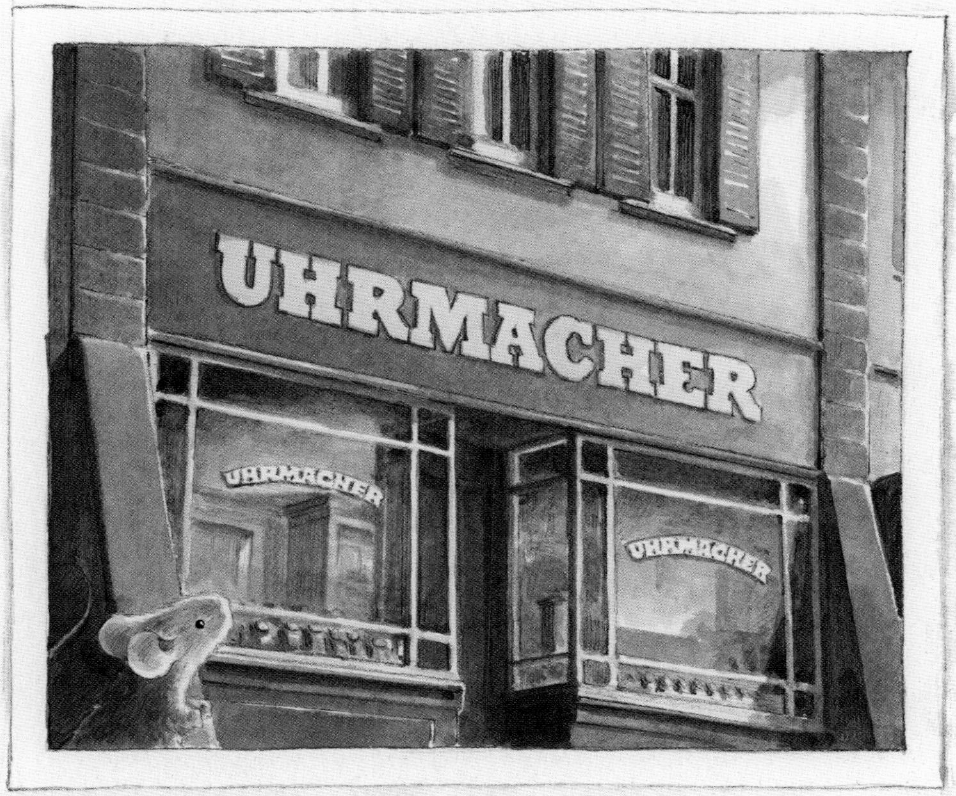
UHRMACHER
UHRMACHER
UHRMACHER

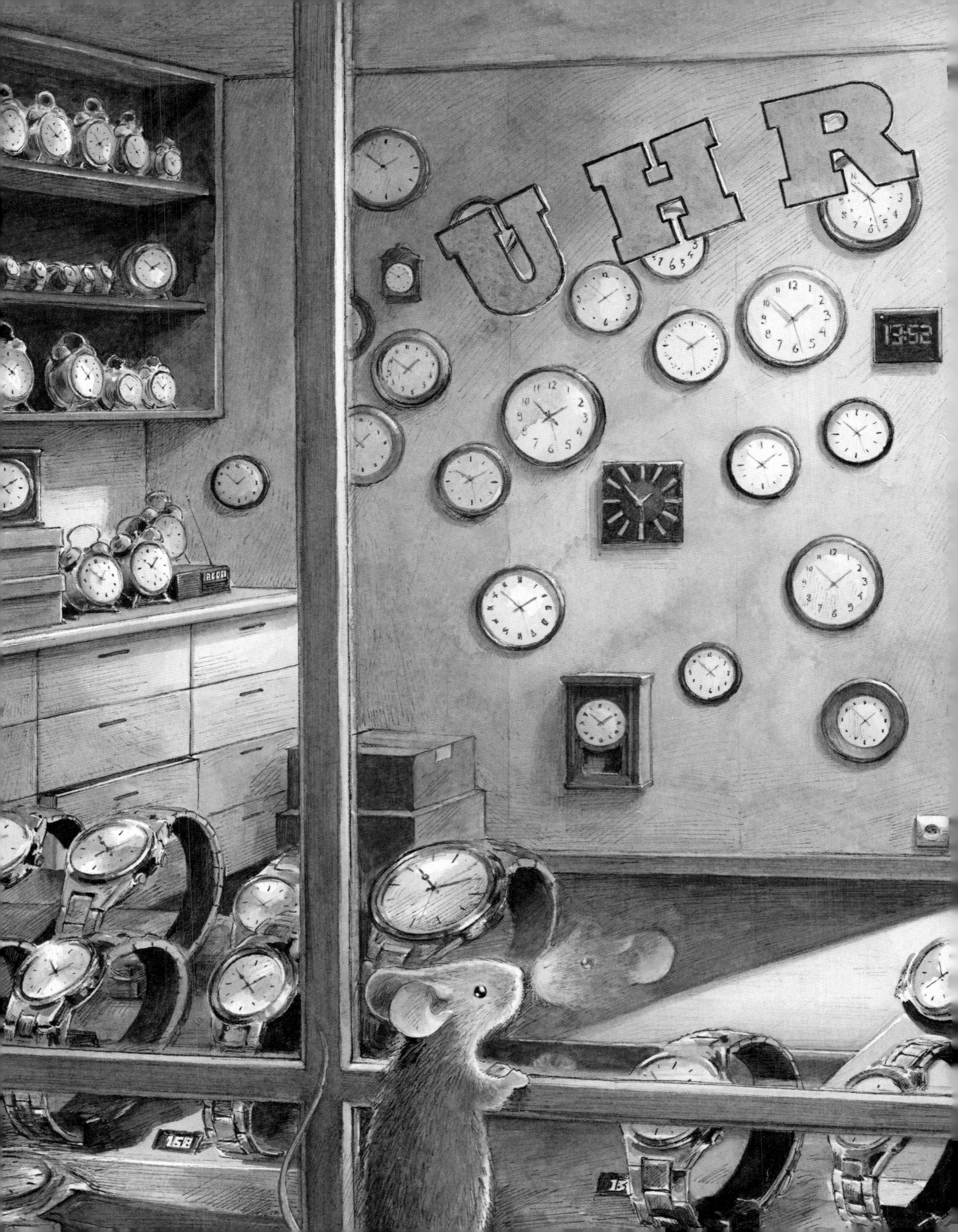
UHR
13:52

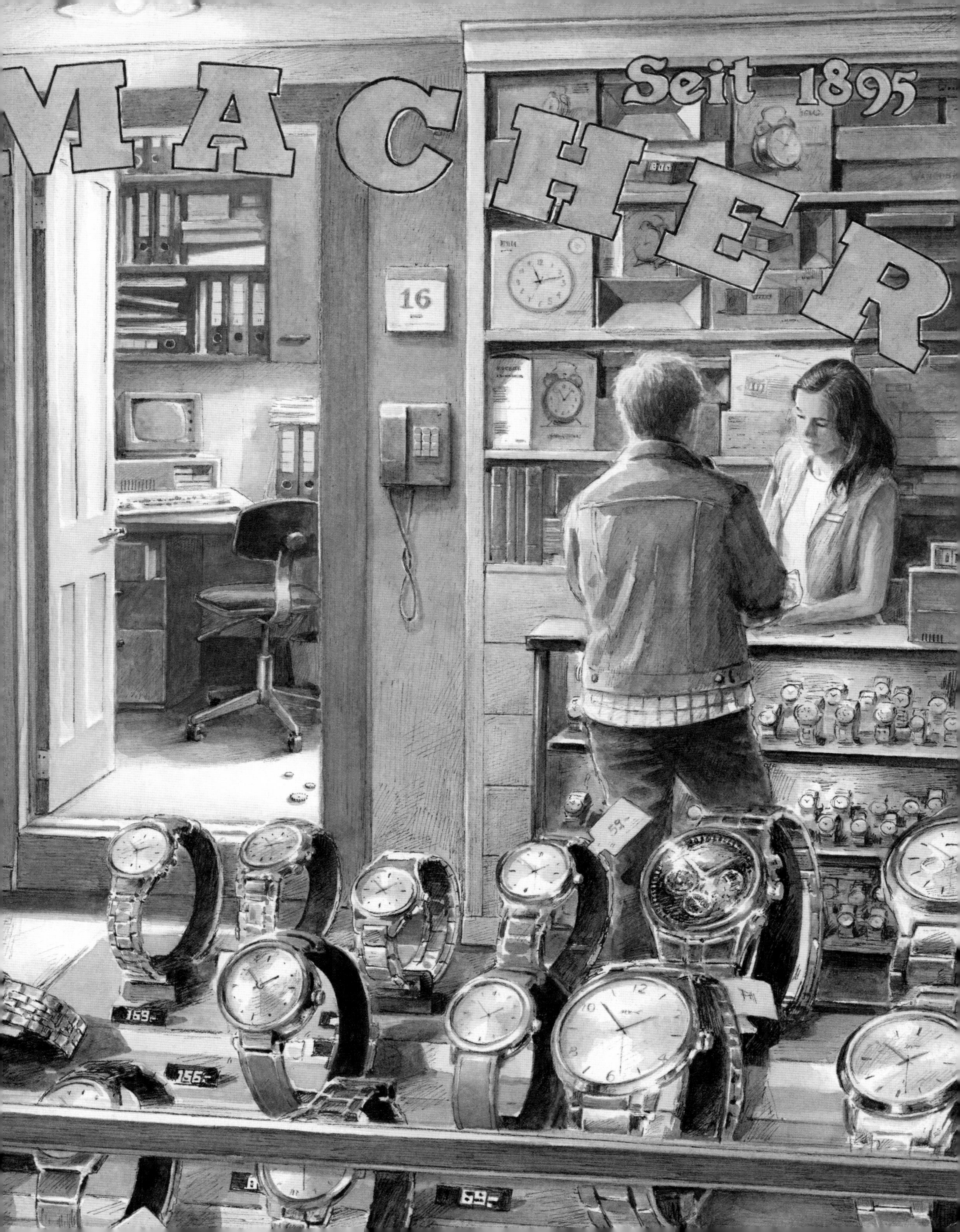
MACHER
Seit 1895
16
159.-
69.-

The clockmaker's workshop

Was that a fellow mouse darting through the shop? Excitedly the little mouse pressed his nose against the cool glass of the window. The snow-white mouse nimbly disappeared into the back of the shop, and he was carrying a few cogwheels.

When a new customer entered the shop, the little mouse scurried in behind him. Then he looked around in astonishment. The shop was full of clocks and watches. There were pocket watches, grandfather clocks, cuckoo clocks, and wristwatches, all accompanied by the familiar ticking and tocking. On a desk in the back room lay catalogs from different manufacturers, and there was a shelf containing a few dusty instruction books on how to repair old grandfather clocks.

Then in a corner behind a heating pipe, barely visible in the darkness, the little mouse discovered tracks. Clearly marked in the thick dust were the paw prints of a mouse. And around another corner, in front of a mouse hole, stood the white mouse.

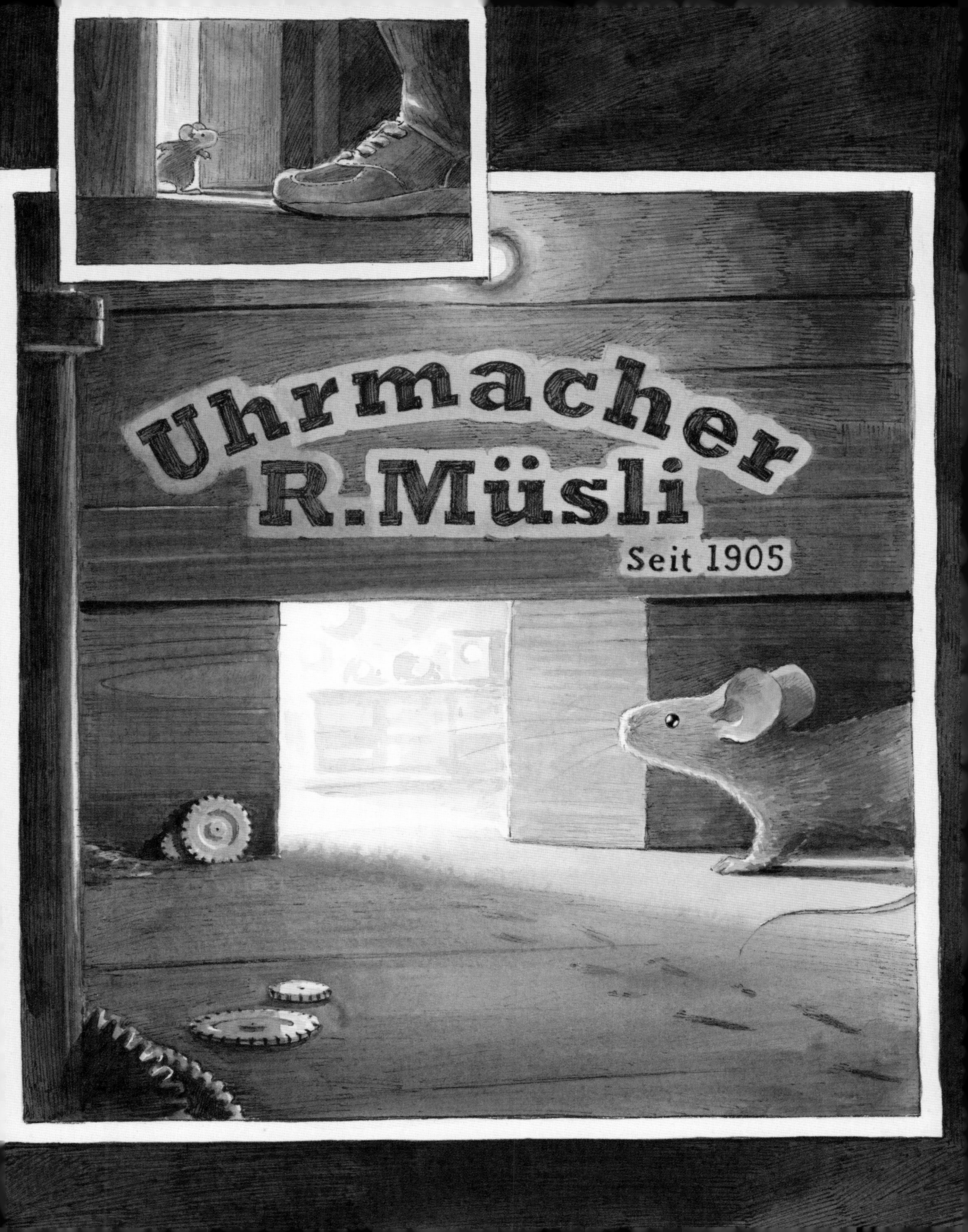
Uhrmacher
R.Müsli
Seit 1905

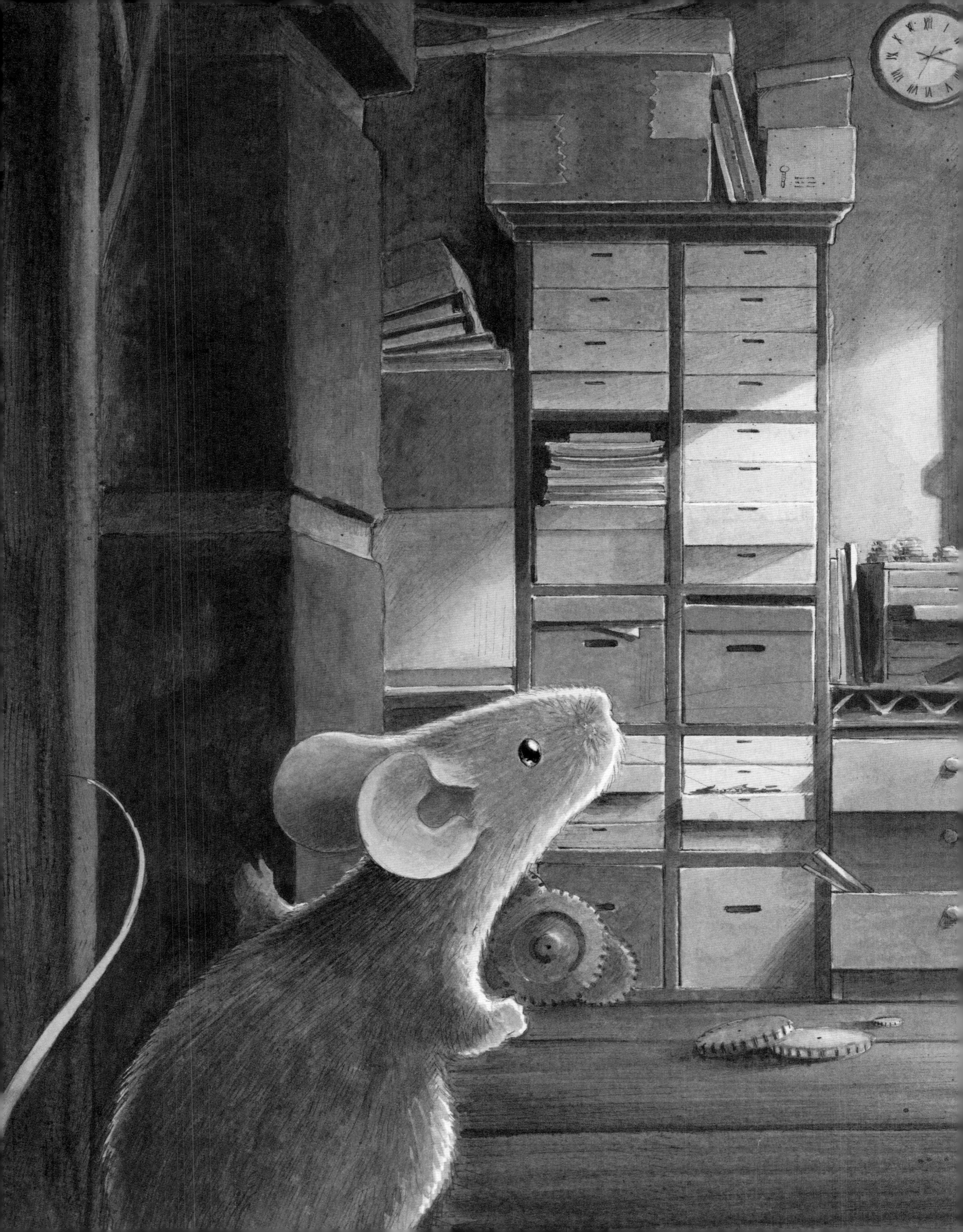

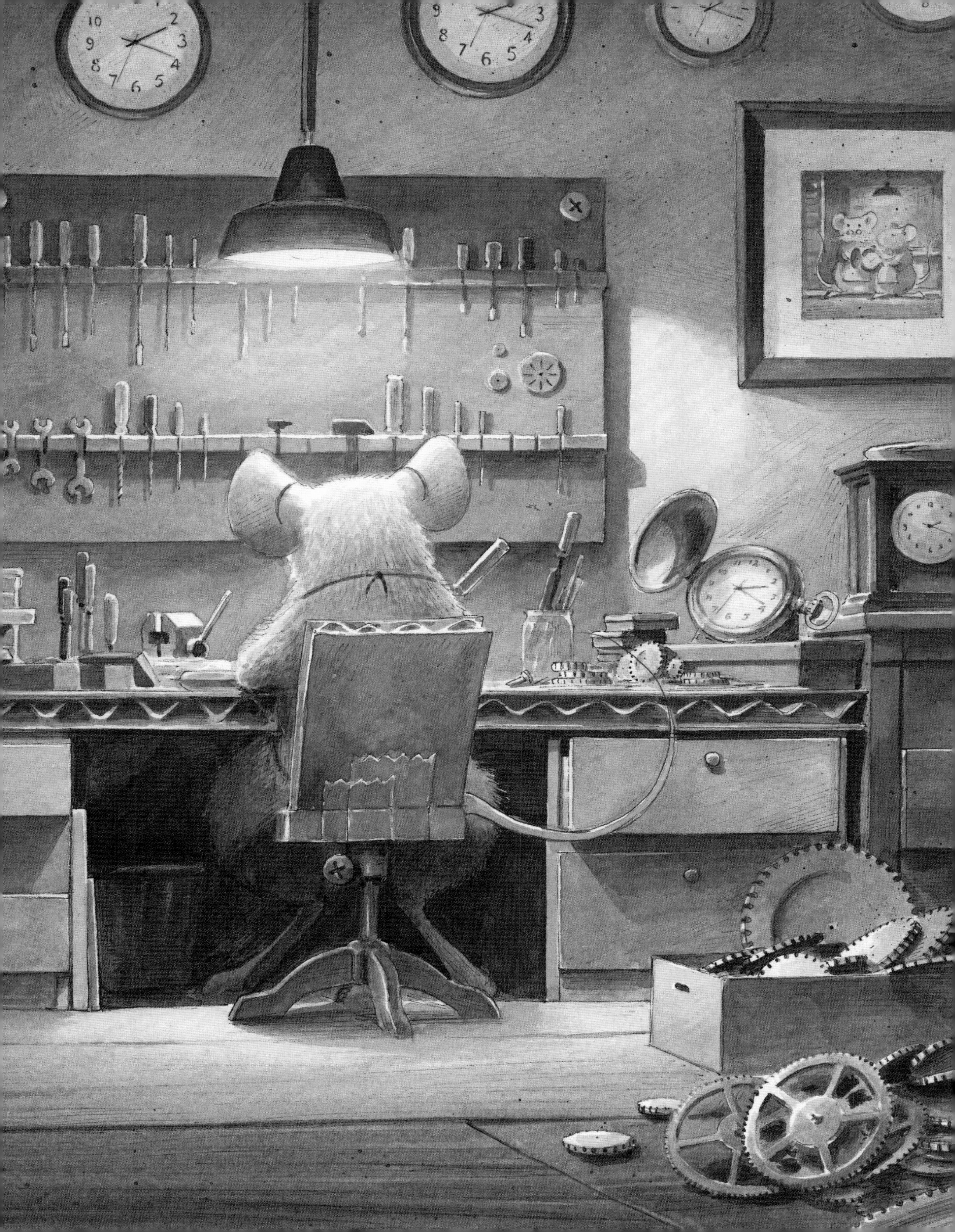

He was leaning over a bench and was completely absorbed in his work. The cogs that he'd been carrying on his back were now leaning against the wall.

"Hello," said the little mouse in a tiny voice. Under no circumstances did he want to startle the other mouse in the midst of whatever he was doing.

"Morning," said the white mouse in a thick Swiss accent without looking up. "Be with you in a moment." He took a tiny screw out of a drawer and used it to attach a cogwheel to the brass object in front of him. "Did it!" He congratulated himself and spent a moment or two admiring his handiwork. Then he turned his attention to the visitor. He had a very strange contraption on his head: a pair of spectacles with magnifying glasses for lenses. "How can I help you?"

"You are a clockmaker, aren't you?" said the little mouse.

"That's right. Are you interested in buying a clock?"

"Well, no, actually I've got a question."

"That's okay. Let's hear it."

The little mouse paused for a moment, trying to think of the best way to form his question. Then he finally asked it. "What is . . . *time*?"

"Do you want to know the time?"

"No, no. I'd like to know what *time* actually is."

The clockmaker looked at him in surprise. No one had ever asked him this question before. The white mouse stroked the white hairs of his little white beard.

Then he beckoned to his visitor. "Come with me."

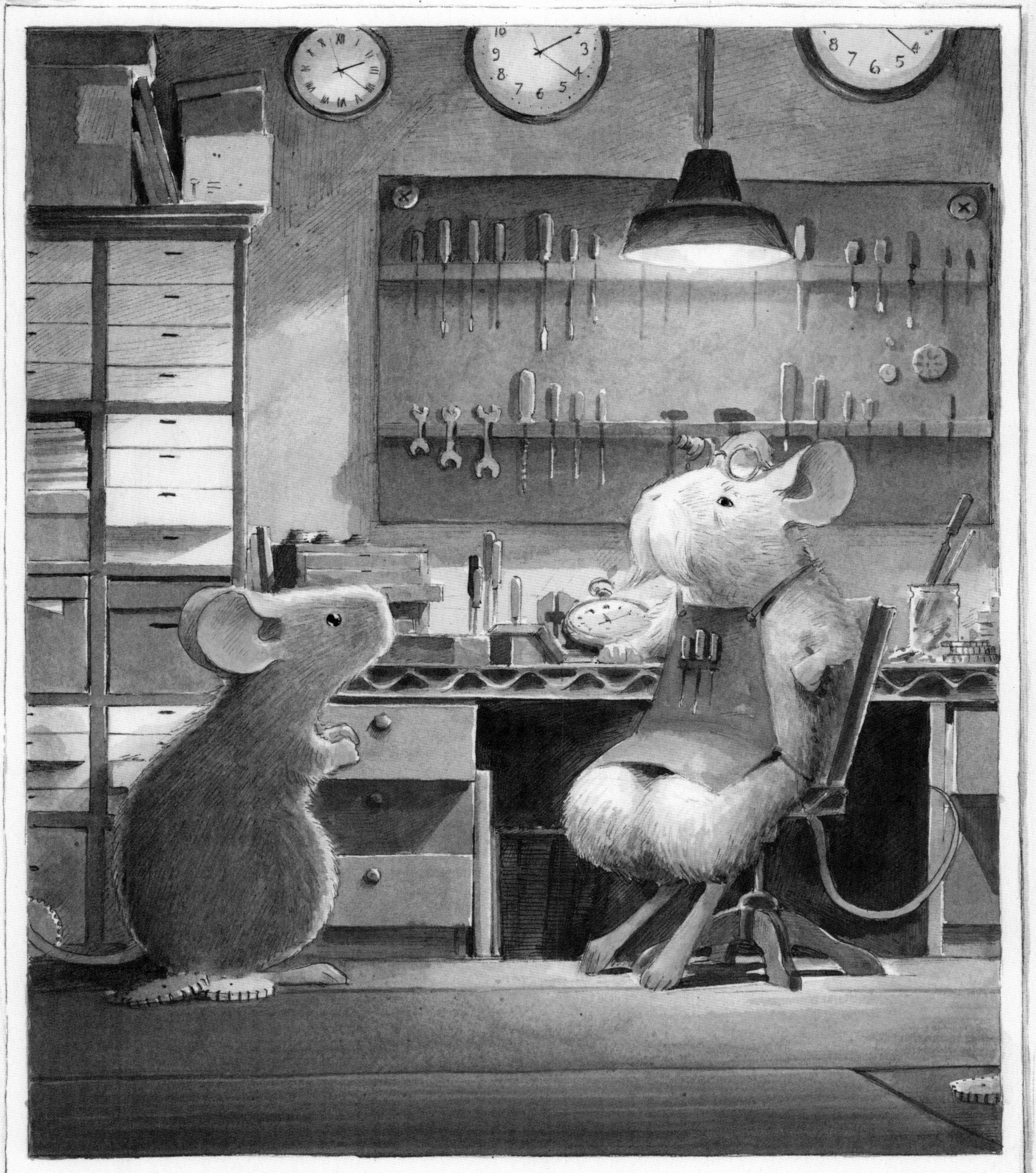

A short history of time

The clockmaker took the little mouse through his workshop. At the back were his collected treasures. Wall clocks no bigger than matchboxes and pocket watches that really would fit into mouse pockets. But there were also other things hanging on the walls or standing on the floor: glass cylinders that tapered toward the middle and were partly filled with sand, and flat disks with numbers on them and a metal rod in the center. A lot of them were rather dusty.

The clockmaker stood in the middle of this collection, cleared his throat, and proudly announced, "Time is my profession. I am happy to tell you everything I have learned about time during all my years as a clockmaker."

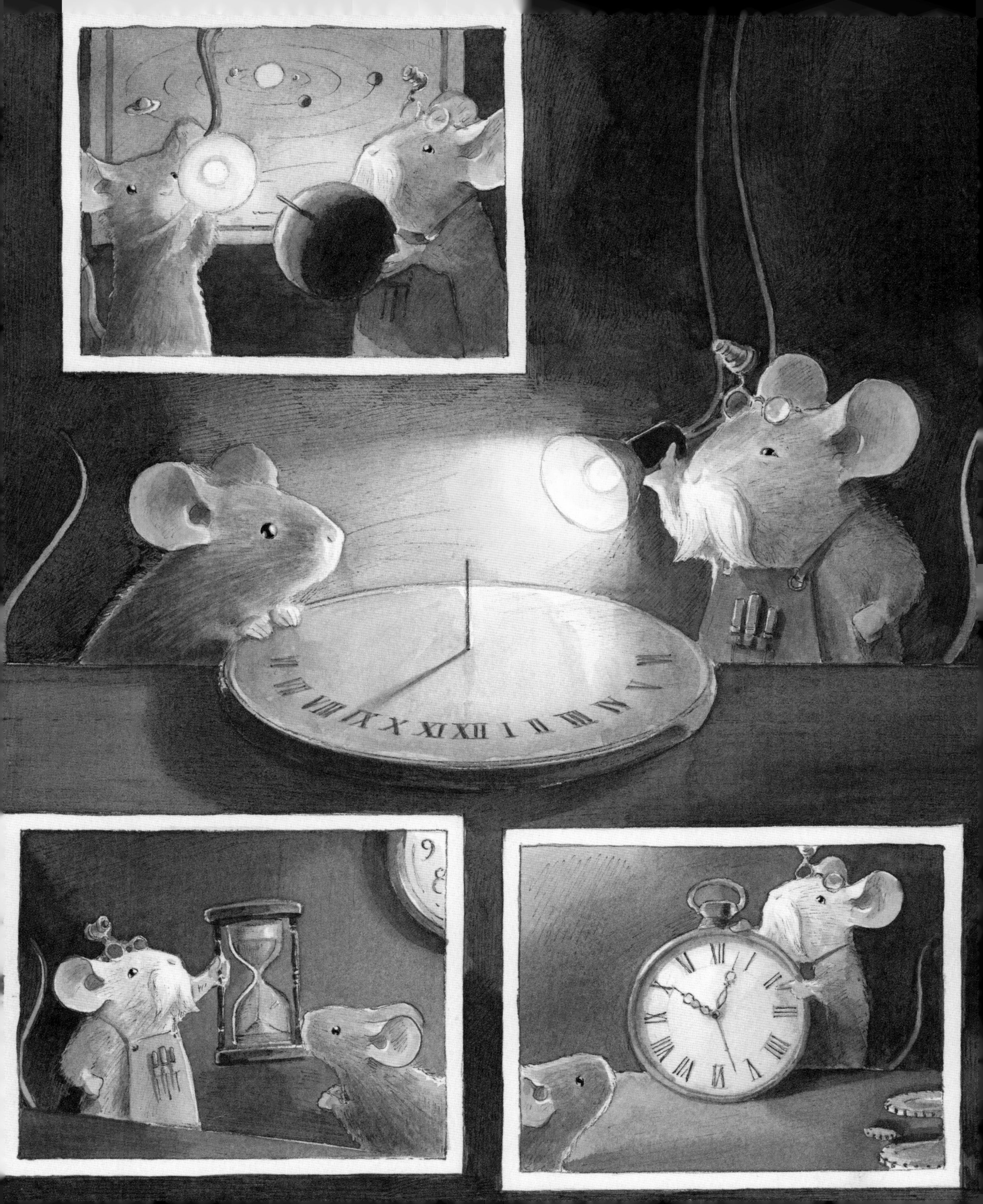

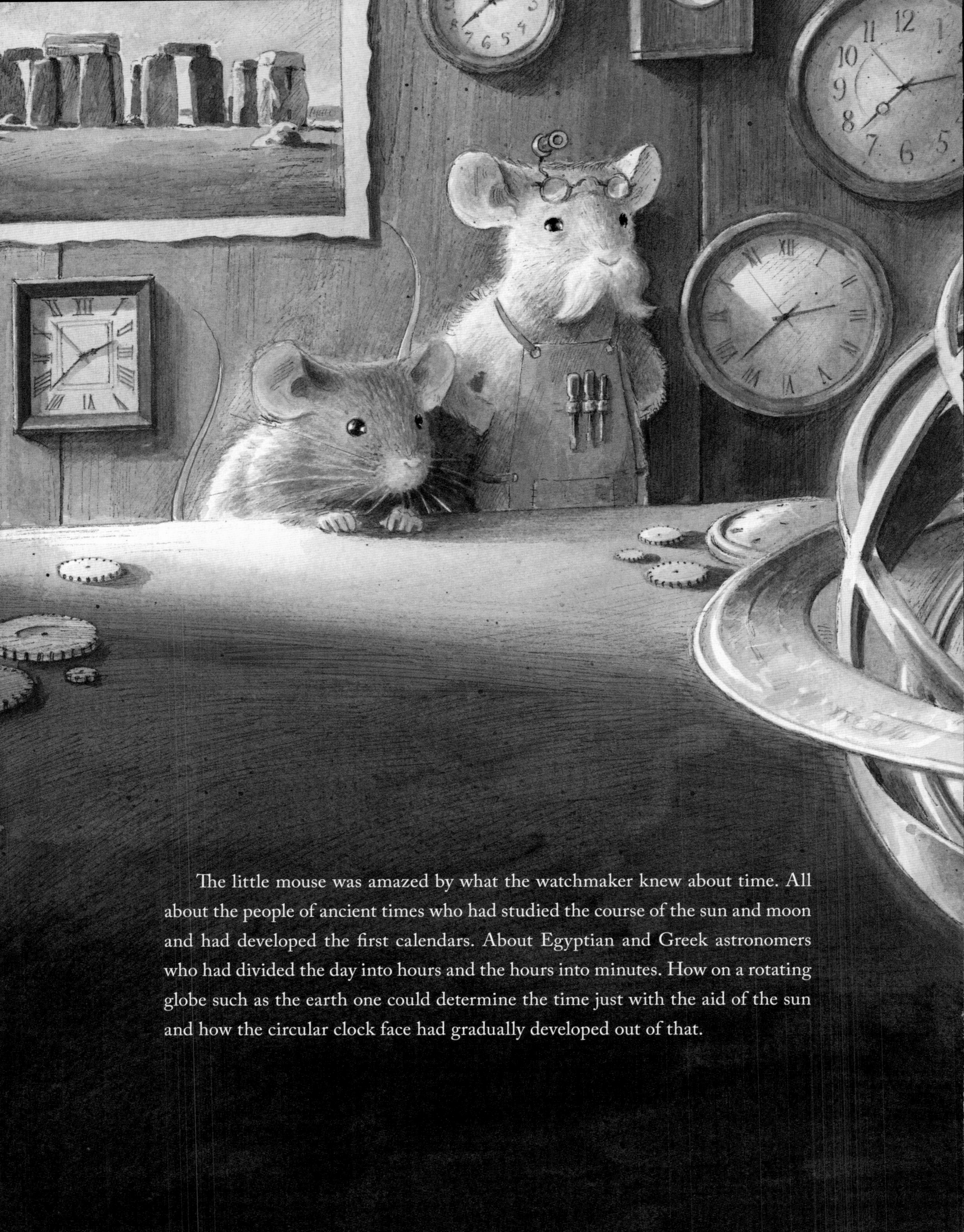

The little mouse was amazed by what the watchmaker knew about time. All about the people of ancient times who had studied the course of the sun and moon and had developed the first calendars. About Egyptian and Greek astronomers who had divided the day into hours and the hours into minutes. How on a rotating globe such as the earth one could determine the time just with the aid of the sun and how the circular clock face had gradually developed out of that.

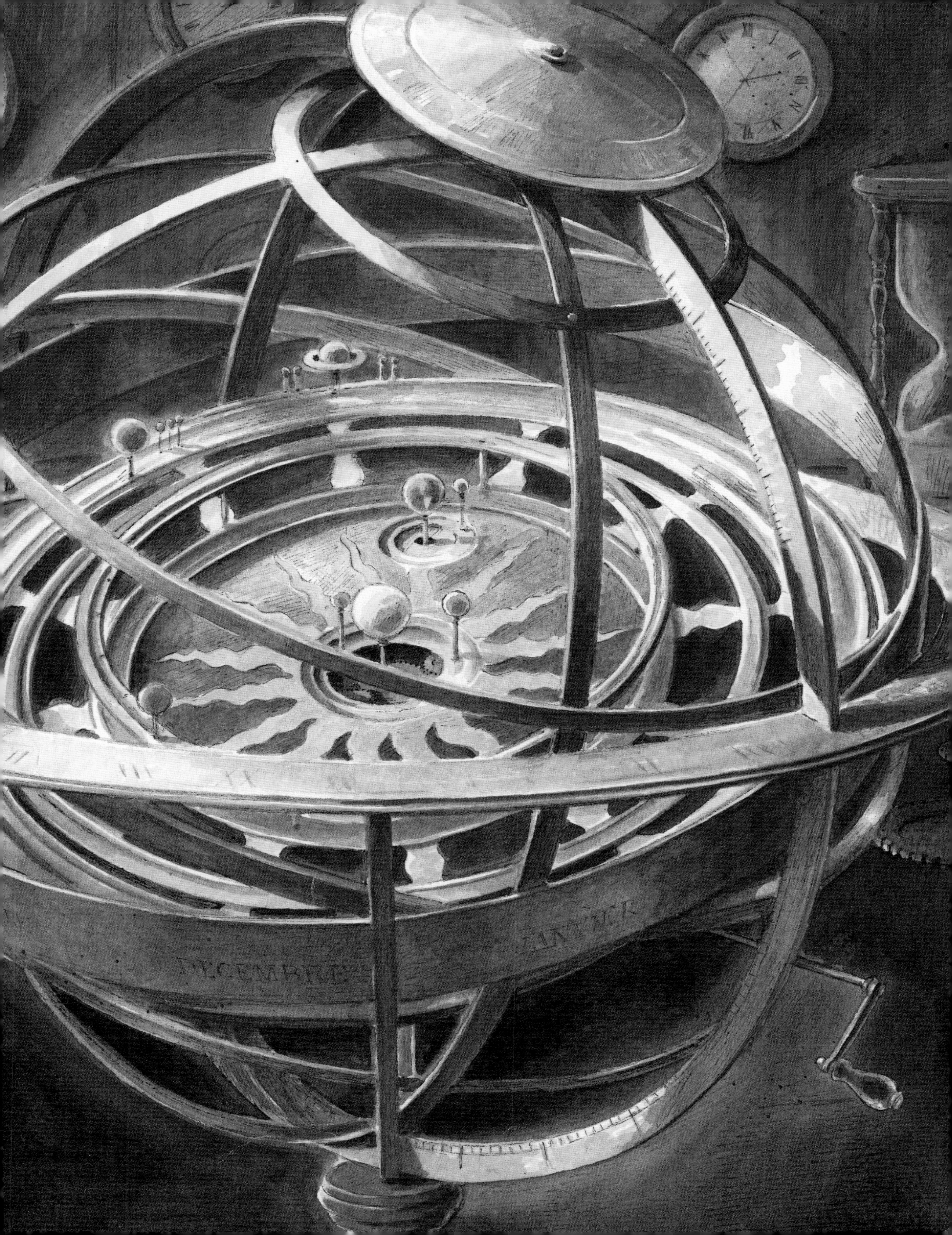
DECEMBRE

"Thank you!" said the little mouse when the two of them returned to the clockmaker's workshop. "You really do know everything about clocks. But tell me, how does a mouse actually get to be a clockmaker?"

"Ah, that's also an interesting story," said the white mouse proudly, and he pointed to some faded photographs on the wall. "We've been clockmakers for generations. My family moved here more than eighty years ago. In those days this place was thought to be extremely dangerous. No mouse dared even to enter the shop. There was a monster living here—black as night, with glaring eyes and a vicious temper. Chronos the tomcat."

The description alone made the little mouse shudder.

The clockmaker continued. "One night Chronos was in a particularly bad mood, and he turned the whole shop upside down. After that he disappeared without a trace. Only when my great-grandparents were certain that he would never come back did they set up home here." At this point the white mouse fell silent, lost in his memories.

The little mouse looked at him expectantly. "And then?"

"What? Oh yes." The clockmaker realized that he had not yet answered the actual question. "When my great-grandparents moved in, they found something amazing." He brought out a small box. Inside it, wrapped in a fine cloth, lay a pocket watch. "They found this watch here. As you can see, it's much smaller than any human pocket watch. My great-grandparents were so fascinated by this discovery, they decided from that moment on they would make mouse watches themselves."

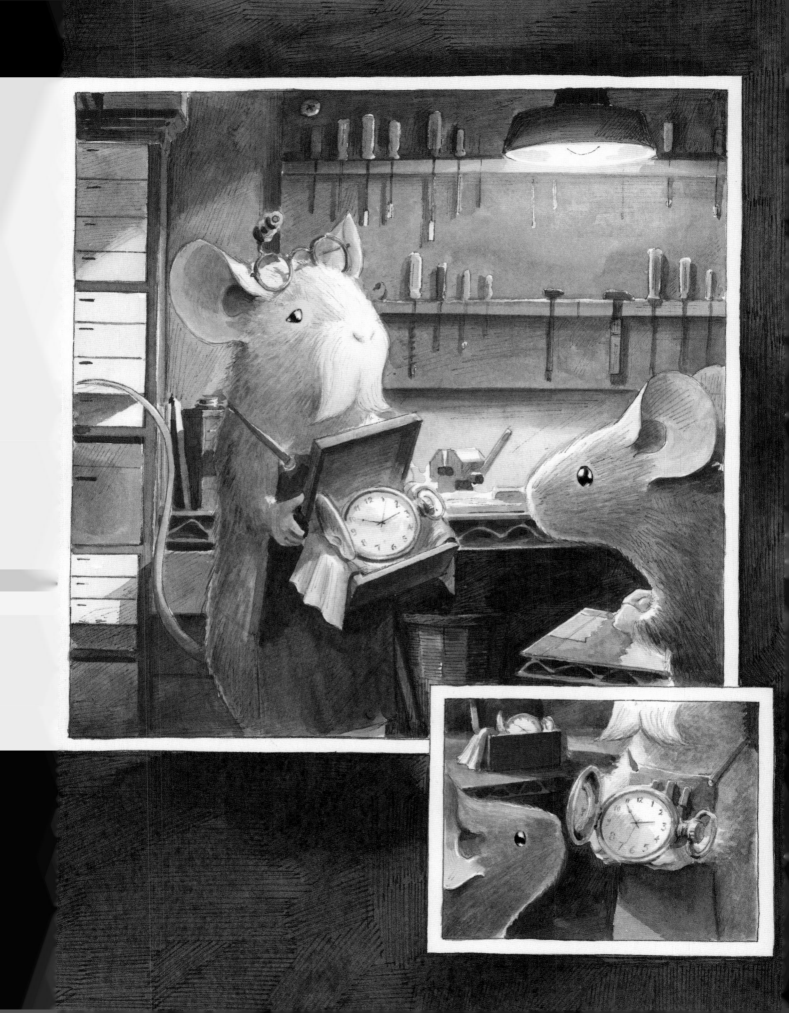

Incredible! The hands were scarcely thicker than a hair. The little mouse gazed at the filigree work on the watch, which was really well preserved. There was nothing to indicate that it was eighty years old. A tiny dent on the brass casing was just about visible. The watch must have fallen down at some time.

"Thank you very much for your time!" said the little mouse, preparing to leave. But when he said the word *time*, it suddenly occurred to him why he had actually come. "Perhaps I could just ask you once more, what exactly *is* time? We haven't spoken about that at all. You see, I'm a day late for something, and I'm looking for a way to reverse time."

"I'm afraid that is a question I can't answer. Time is something that constantly flows in the same direction. Clocks and calendars only help to show us the passing of time. I'm sorry to disappoint you, but I don't have a better answer." For a moment the clockmaker looked a little sad. However, his mood quickly lightened when an idea came into his head. "Please take one of my watches with you," he said, "as a little present. And if you don't succeed in reversing time, at least in the future you will never be late again."

The little mouse was very touched. Now he was the owner of a magnificent pocket watch. It was almost an exact copy of the clockmaker's eighty-year-old watch, but without the dent in the brass casing.

He had almost left the room when the clockmaker came running after him.

"Something else has occurred to me that might help you," he panted. "A good eighty years ago a scientist lived in this town, and if I remember rightly, he had some revolutionary ideas about time."

The patent office

The floorboards were smooth and cold. One door followed another, and they all looked the same. The fluorescent lighting bathed everything in a clinical glow, which mingled with the rays of the sun from outside. There wasn't a human being in sight. Nevertheless, the little mouse crept very cautiously along the corridors. He stopped in front of a large wall. Hanging on it was the framed photograph of a man with a bushy mustache and messy hair. The following text was below the photograph:

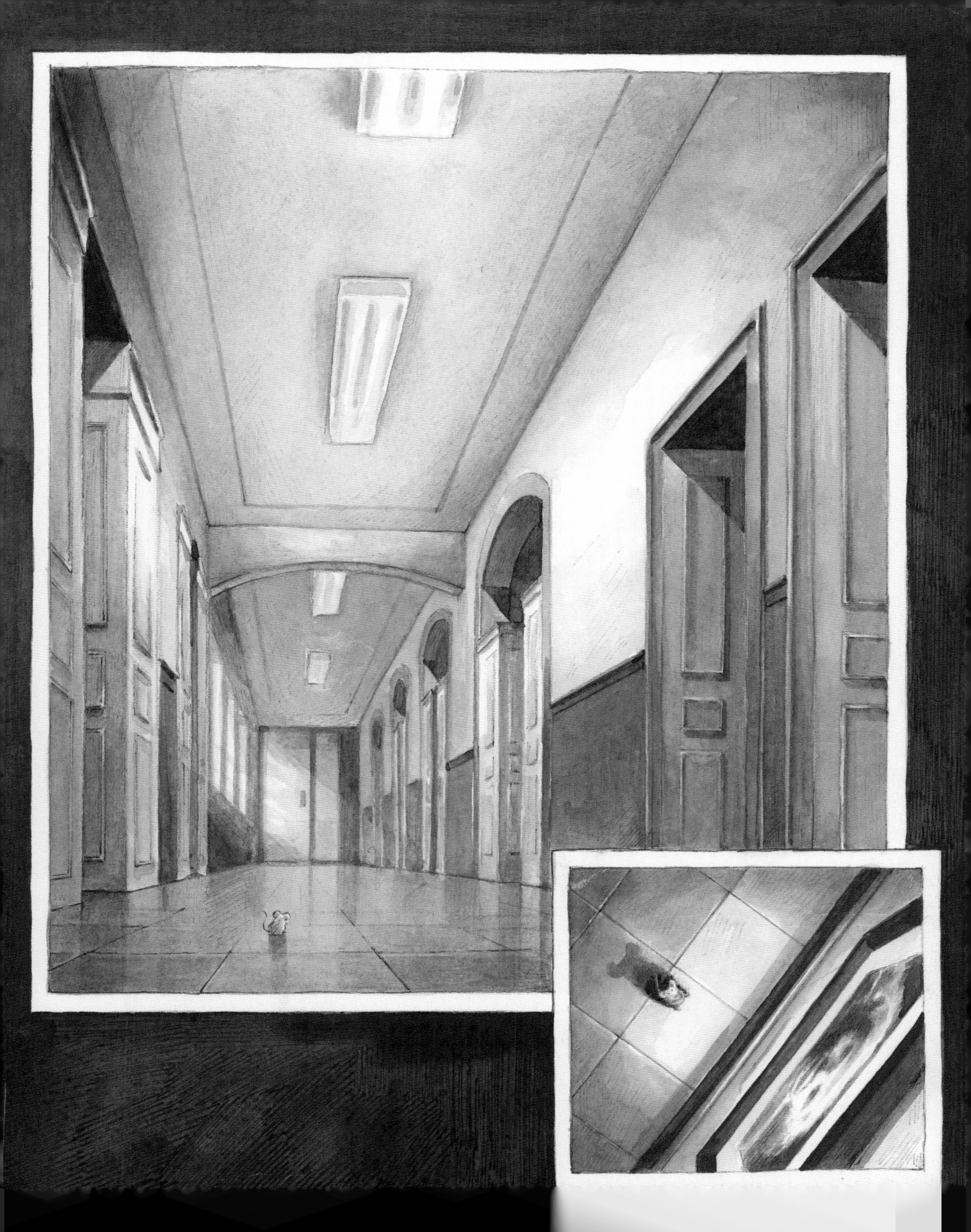

"The physicist and later winner of the Nobel Prize Albert Einstein worked here from 1902 until 1909."

The name seemed familiar to the little mouse. There were a few more sentences about Einstein's life, but he skimmed through them. When he got to the last sentence however, his eyes began to sparkle. "Einstein's work changed forever our concept of space and . . ." He had to look at the last word again just to make sure. Then he whispered it out loud: ". . . *time*!"

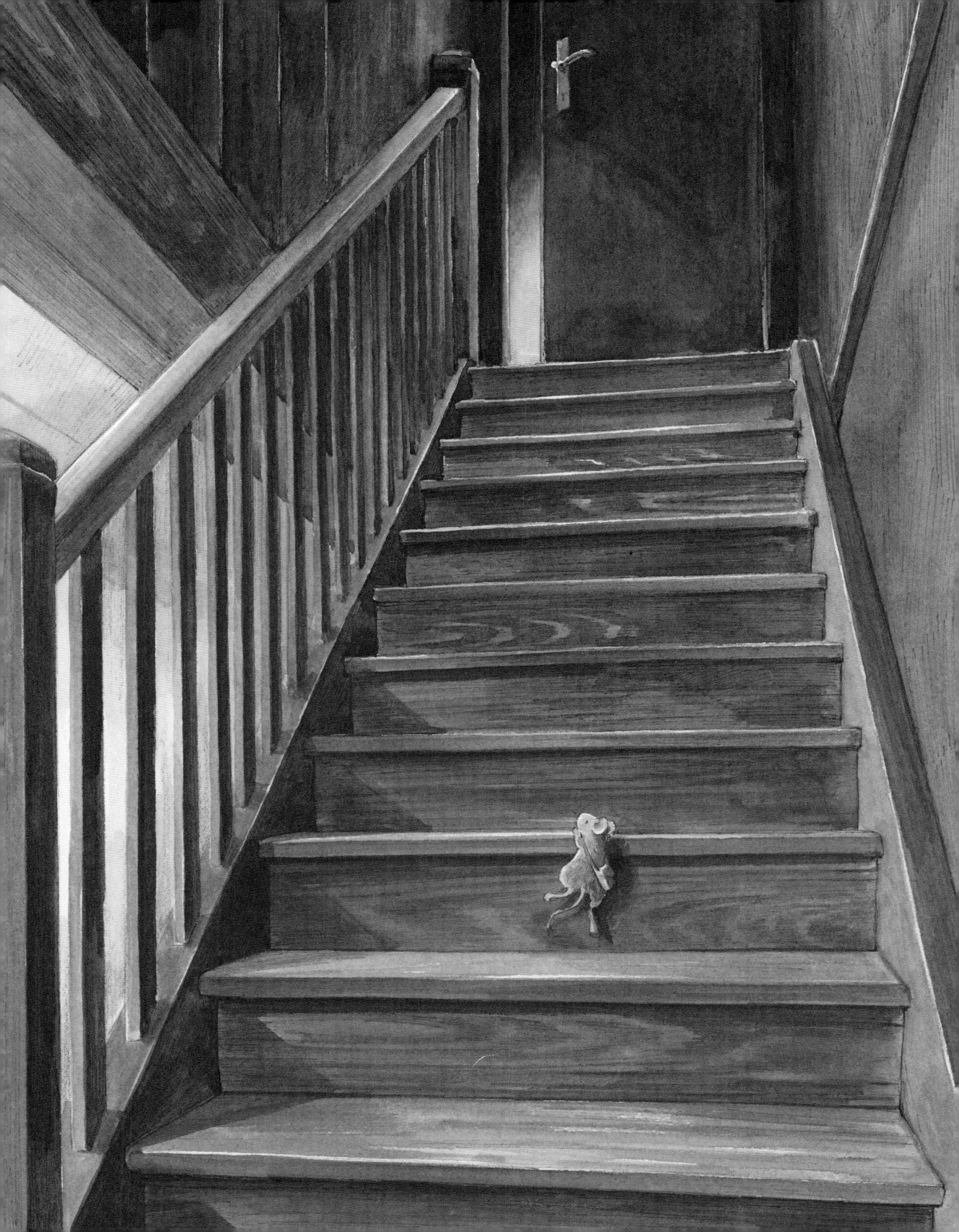

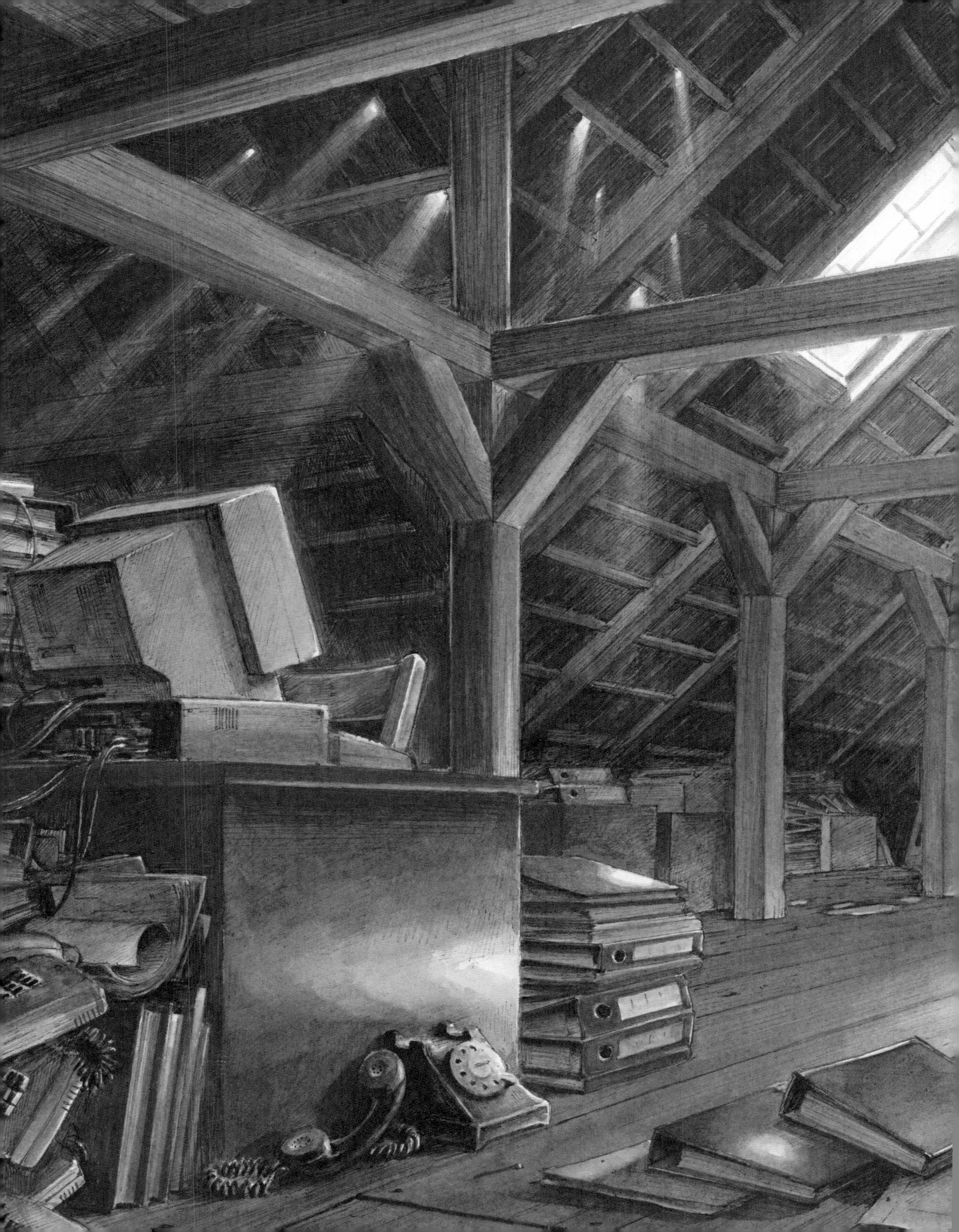

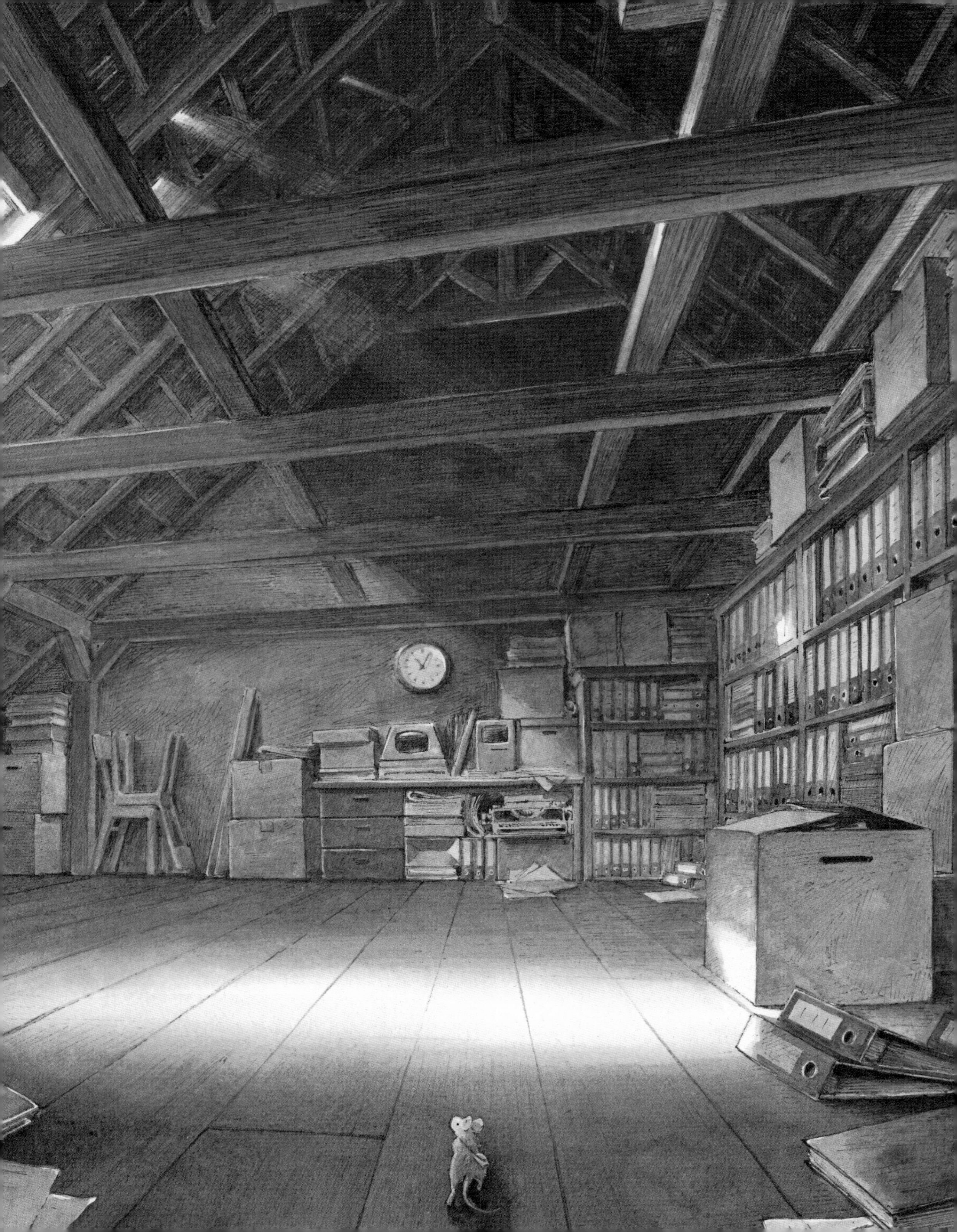

TIME

relativity of time

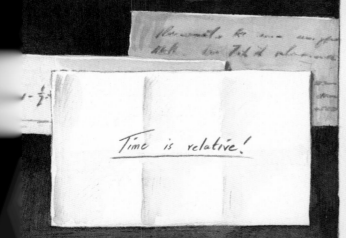

Time is relative!

TIME

The little mouse had now spent several days and nights in the attic of the patent office. All the junk up there made for the best hiding place. Most of the shelves were bulging with old files and masses of paper. There was only one cupboard containing a few dusty books, and among these was a history of the city of Bern. But the most interesting book was a thick clothbound volume, worn at the edges. On the spine, in small letters, was the name *Albert Einstein* and in larger letters *Theory of General Relativity.*

For days on end the little mouse did nothing but read this book. And he learned amazing things. Such as how electromagnetism affected the planets and all about the speed of light. According to Einstein, even the passage of time was *relative*. The speed at which time passed depended on the proverbial eye of the beholder.

But all these profound insights and mathematical formulas gave no clue as to how time might be reversed. Time could be slowed down, accelerated, or even stopped—but it couldn't be reversed. To his great disappointment, the little mouse had to acknowledge that apparently a journey into the past was not possible. He reached out to put the heavy clothbound book back on its shelf.

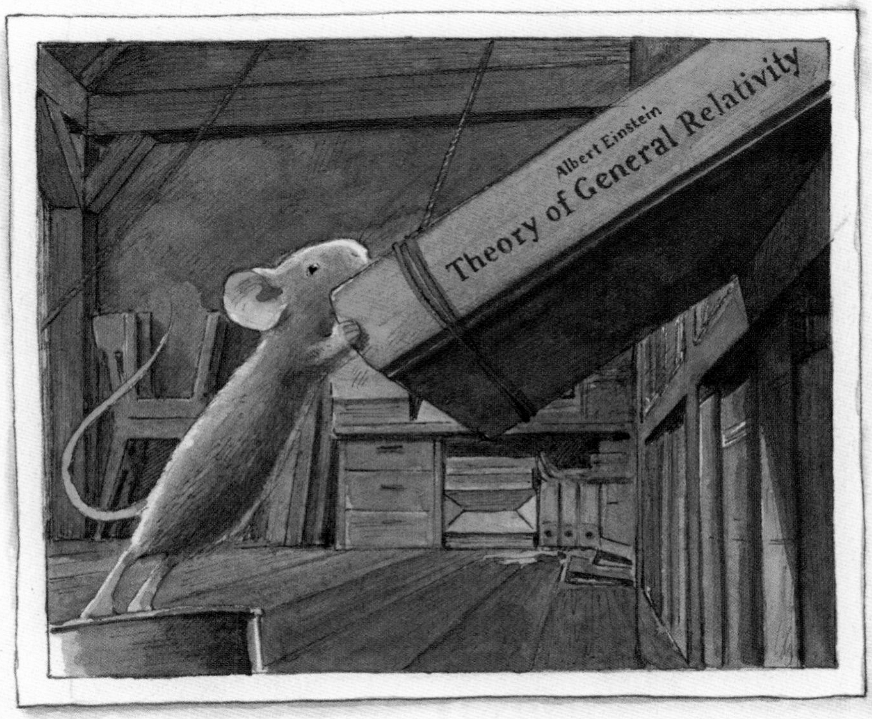
Albert Einstein
Theory of General Relativity

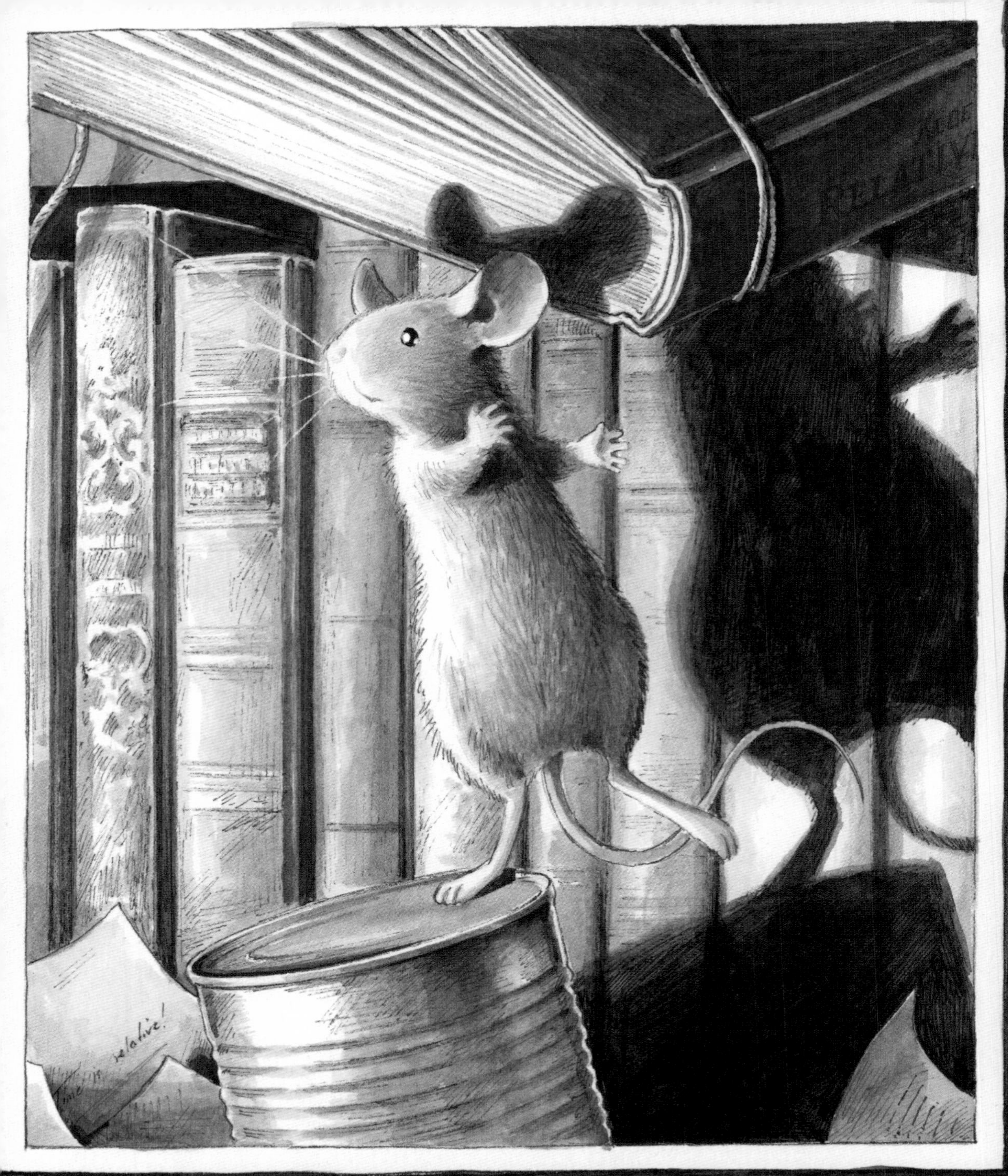
Time is relative!

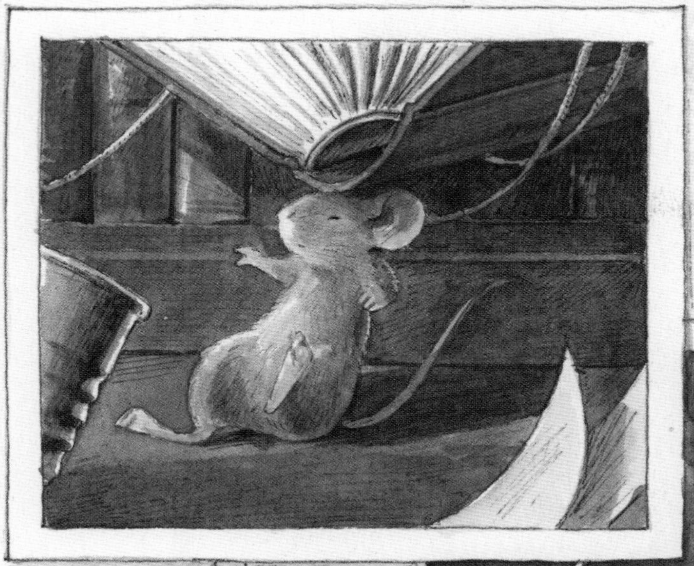

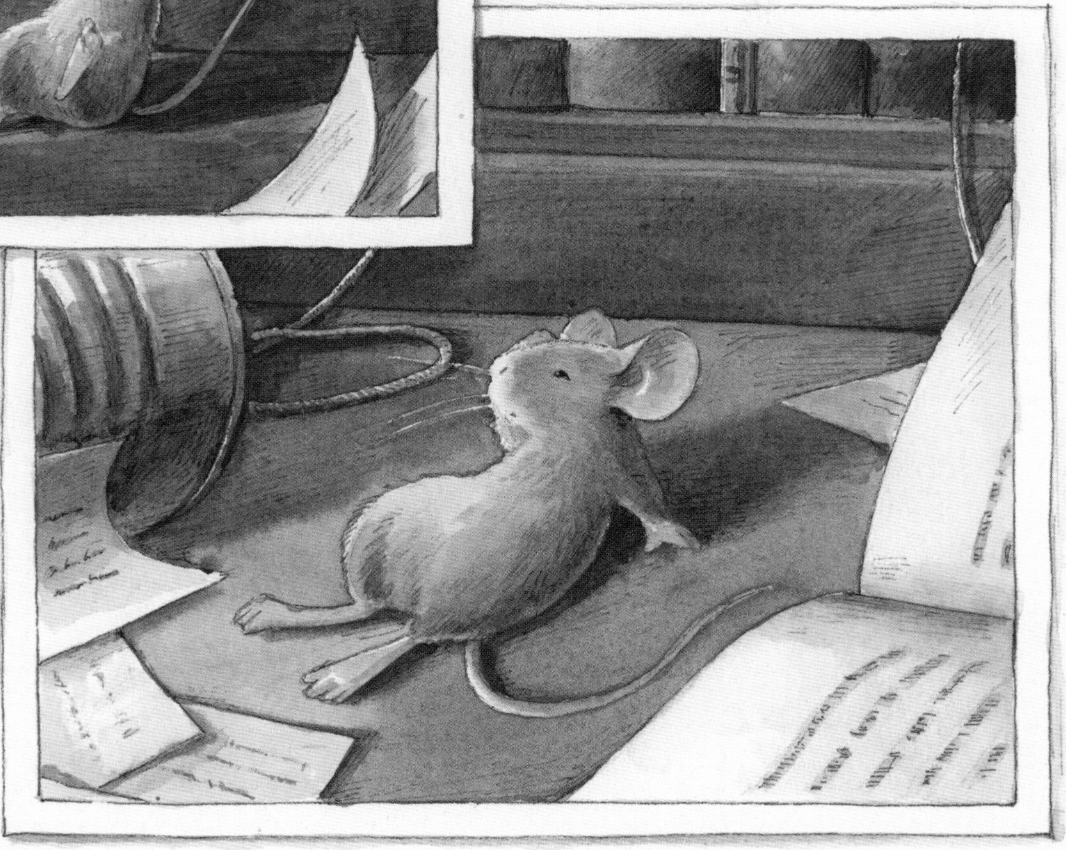

What had happened? A bolt of lightning? The little mouse was still trembling. He had been given a terrible fright and had lost his balance. The book that he had just been trying, with all his strength, to heave back onto its shelf had hit him on the head. Now, still dazed, he looked around. The book lay open next to him. And suddenly thoughts began to flood into his brain. Eureka! Cleverly concealed among Einstein's equations, long rows of figures, and mathematical signs, the little mouse made an amazing discovery.

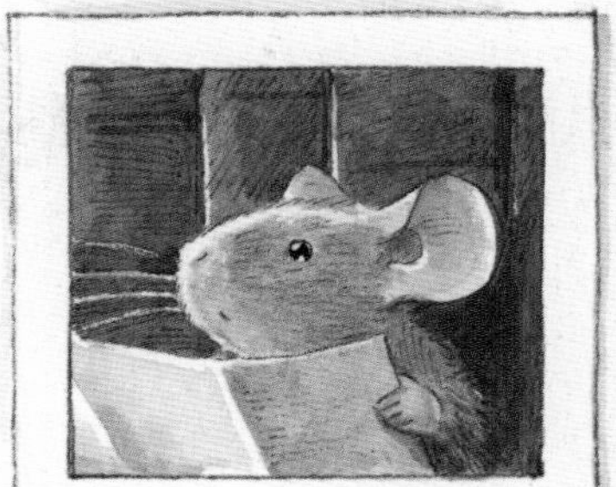

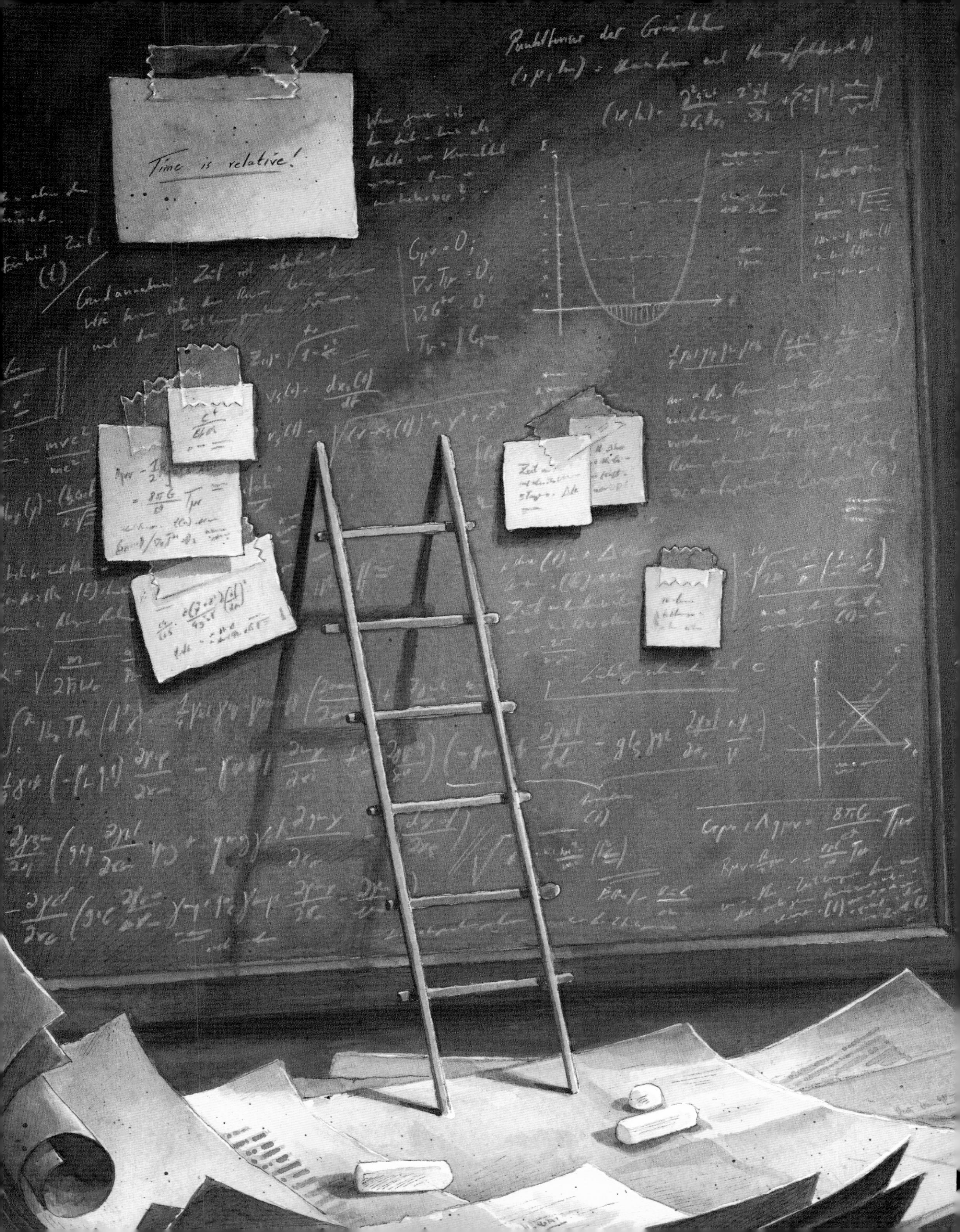
Time is relative!

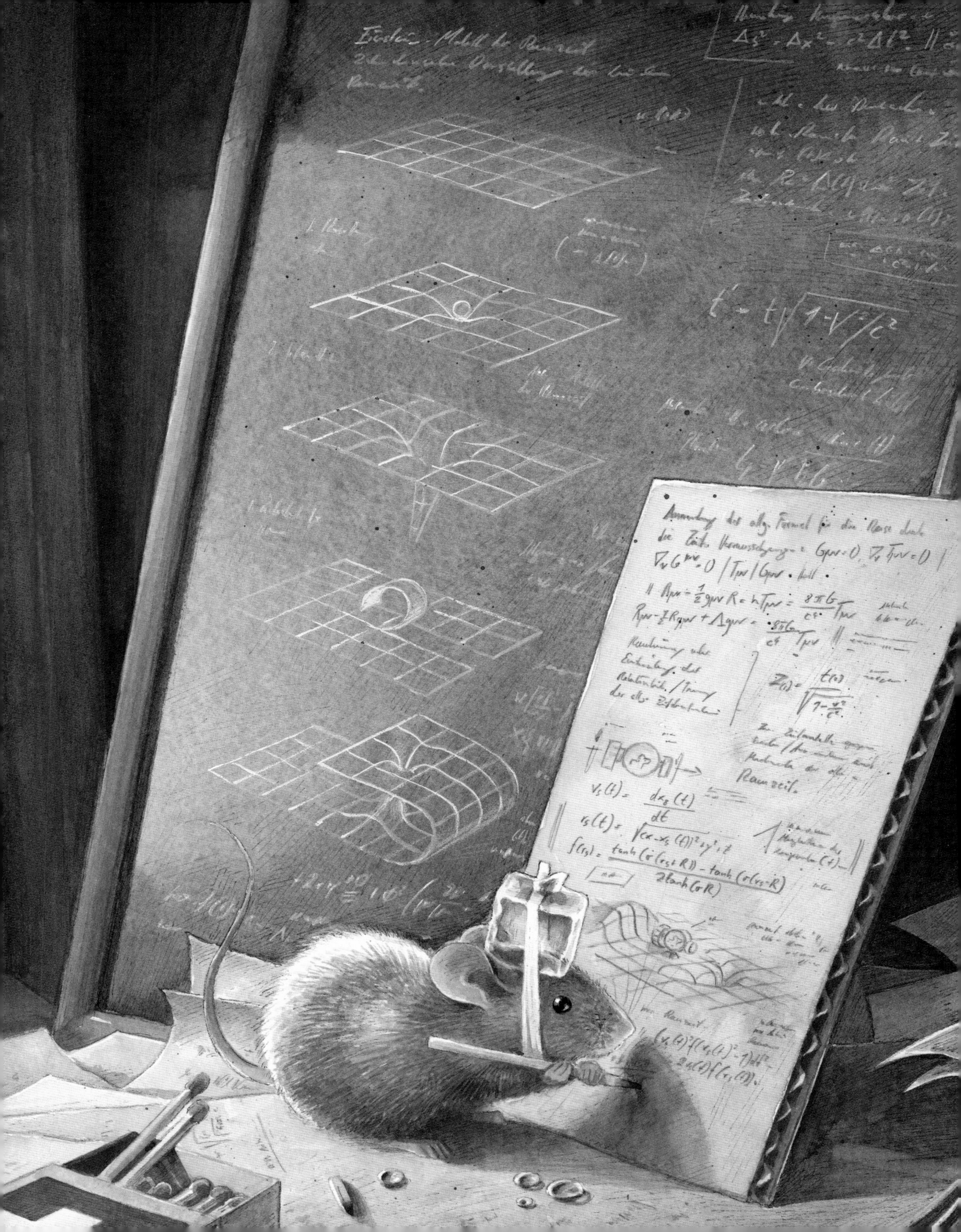
Raumzeit.

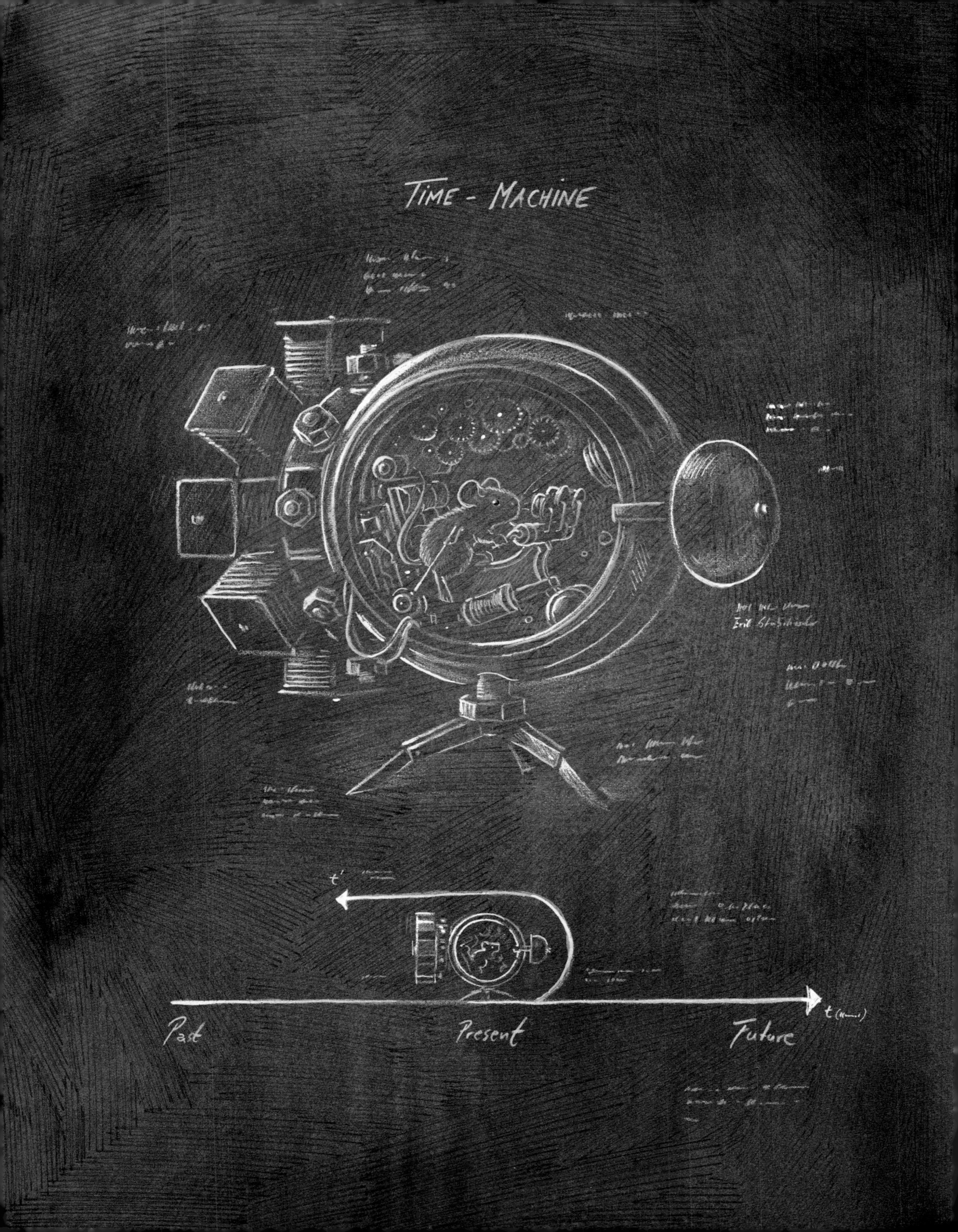
TIME - MACHINE
t'
t
Past
Present
Future

A way through time

At a single stroke everything had become clear. The blow to the head had given the mouse the missing information about how to construct a machine that could travel back through time. Or would it be more of a controlled falling out of time? His brain started to formulate the first calculations, even though his head was still throbbing and a little bump was forming. Undeterred, after he had noted the final figures, the mouse began to work out plans for his invention. For the basic framework he would need a solid metal casing. "What could be better than an alarm clock?" he asked himself, and so he drew a rounded shape. In the middle of this he drew the pilot's seat, with various handles, levers, and wheels.

Armed with a long list of components, the little mouse now mounted a series of raids on the houses of the humans. Of course, he already knew where to find a suitable alarm clock.

After just a few days he had a considerable collection of parts for his machine. The floor of the attic in the patent office was now covered with different-colored wires, copper coils, screws, cogwheels, and bits of computers. It was time to put them all together.

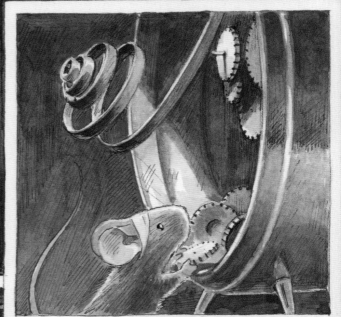

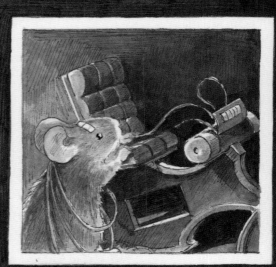

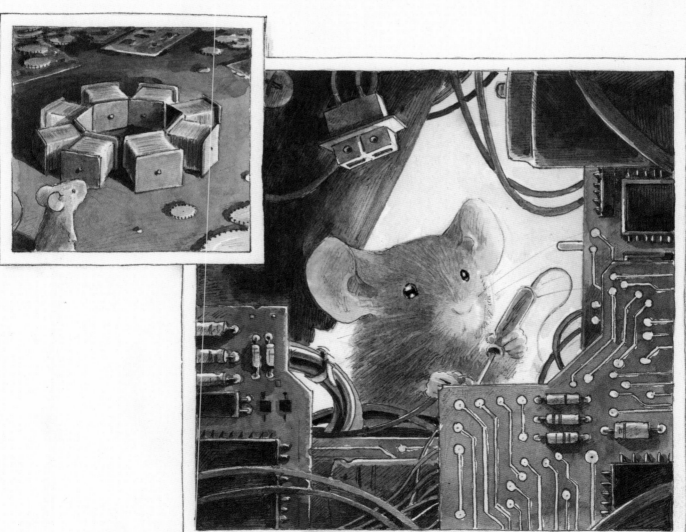

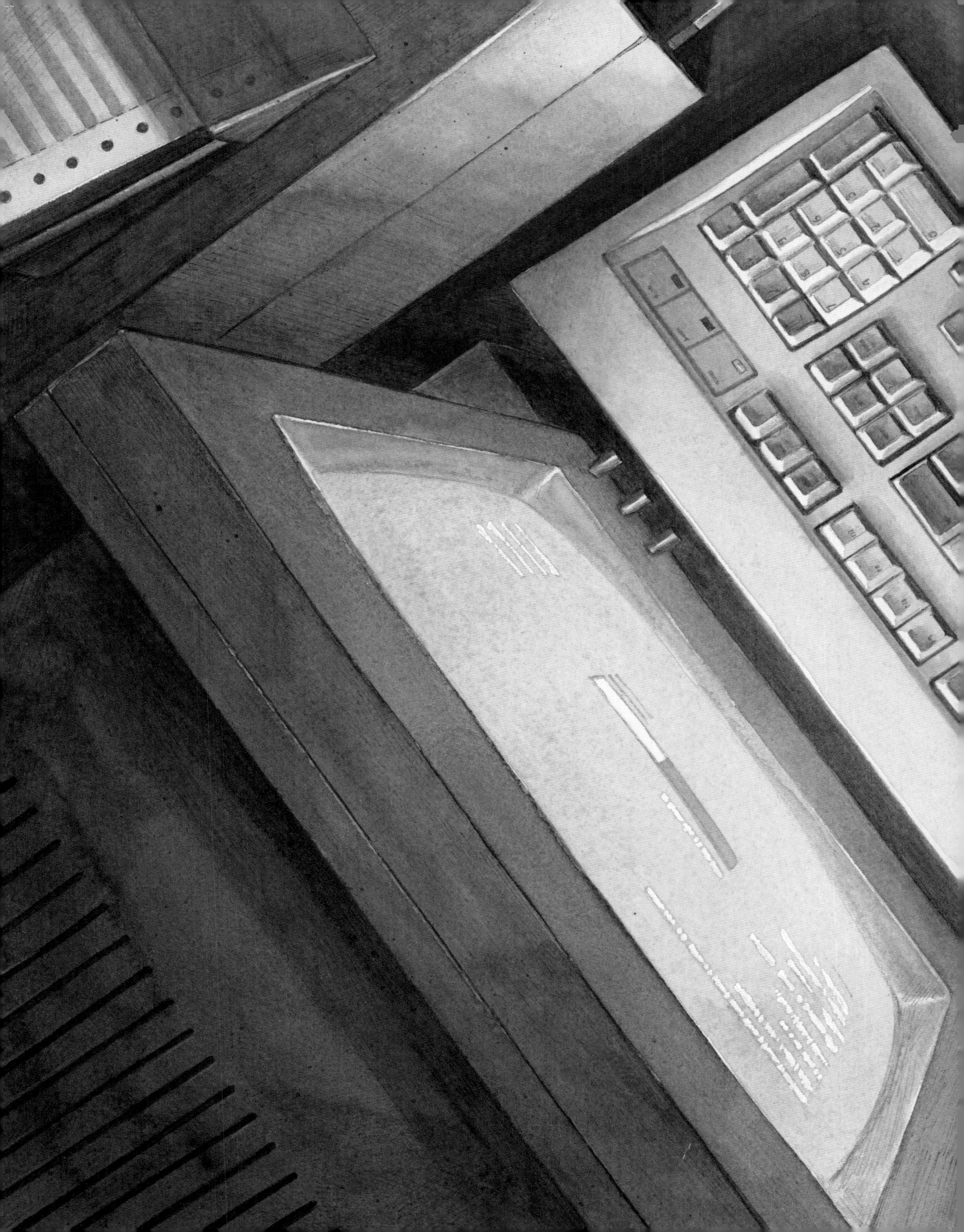

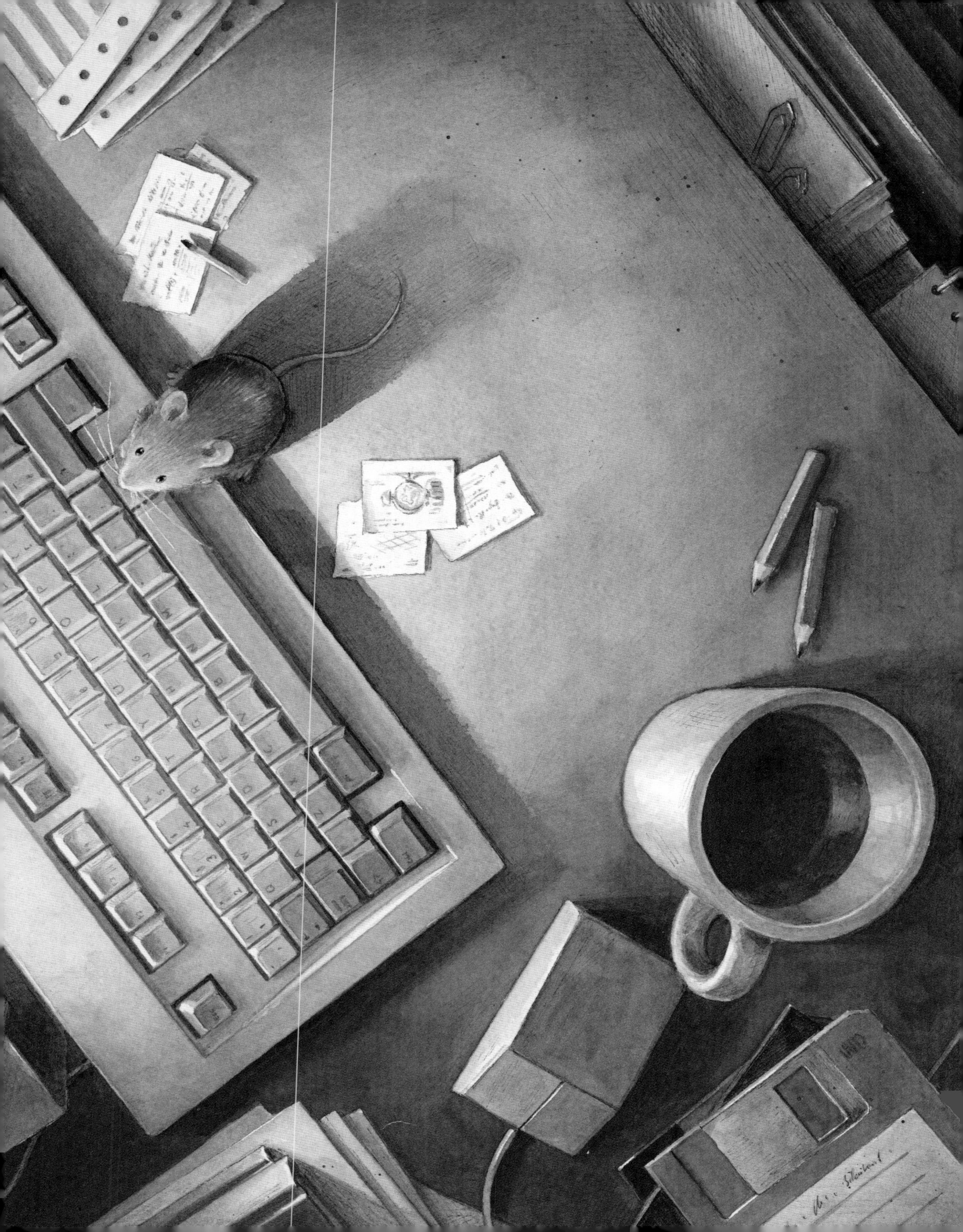

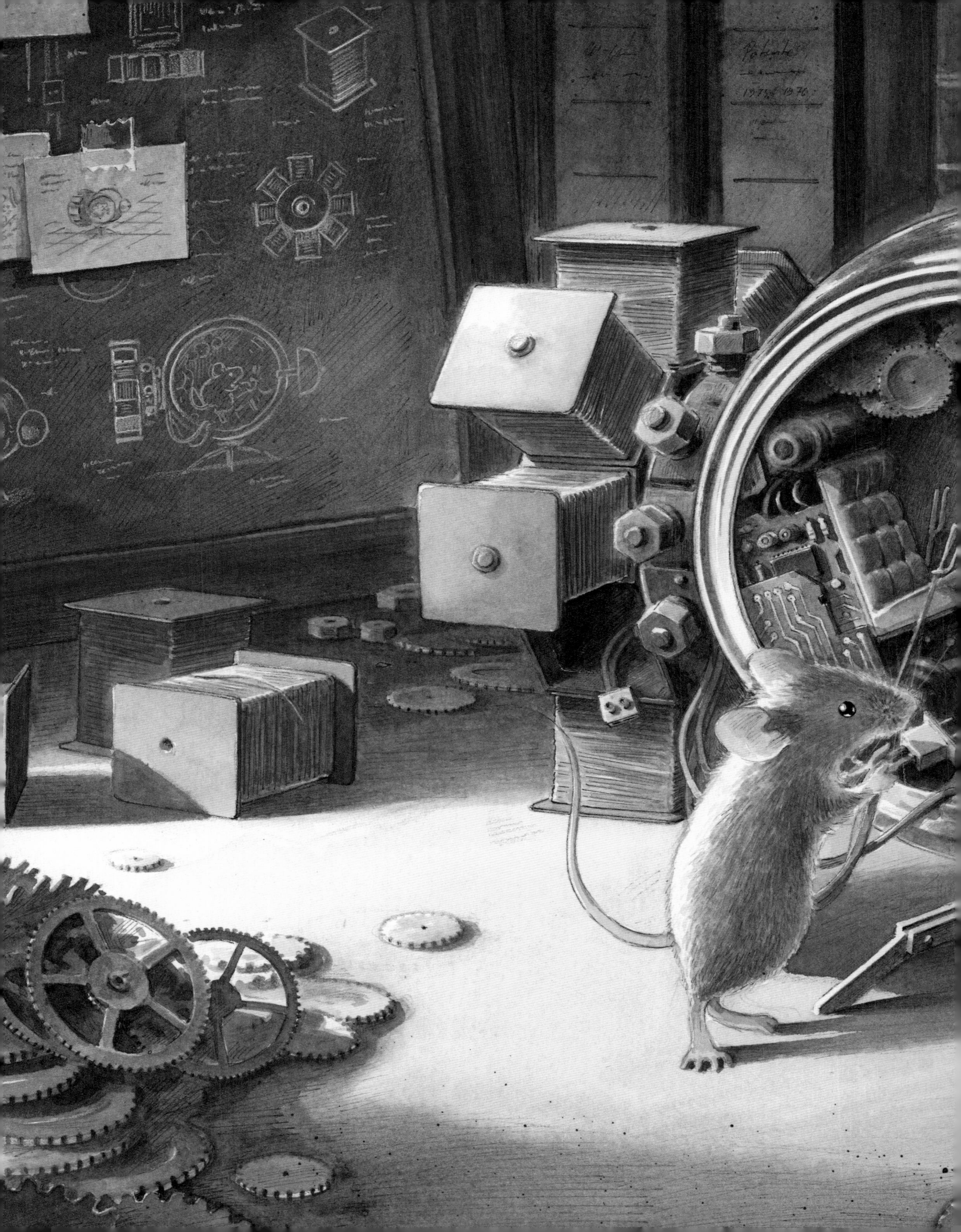

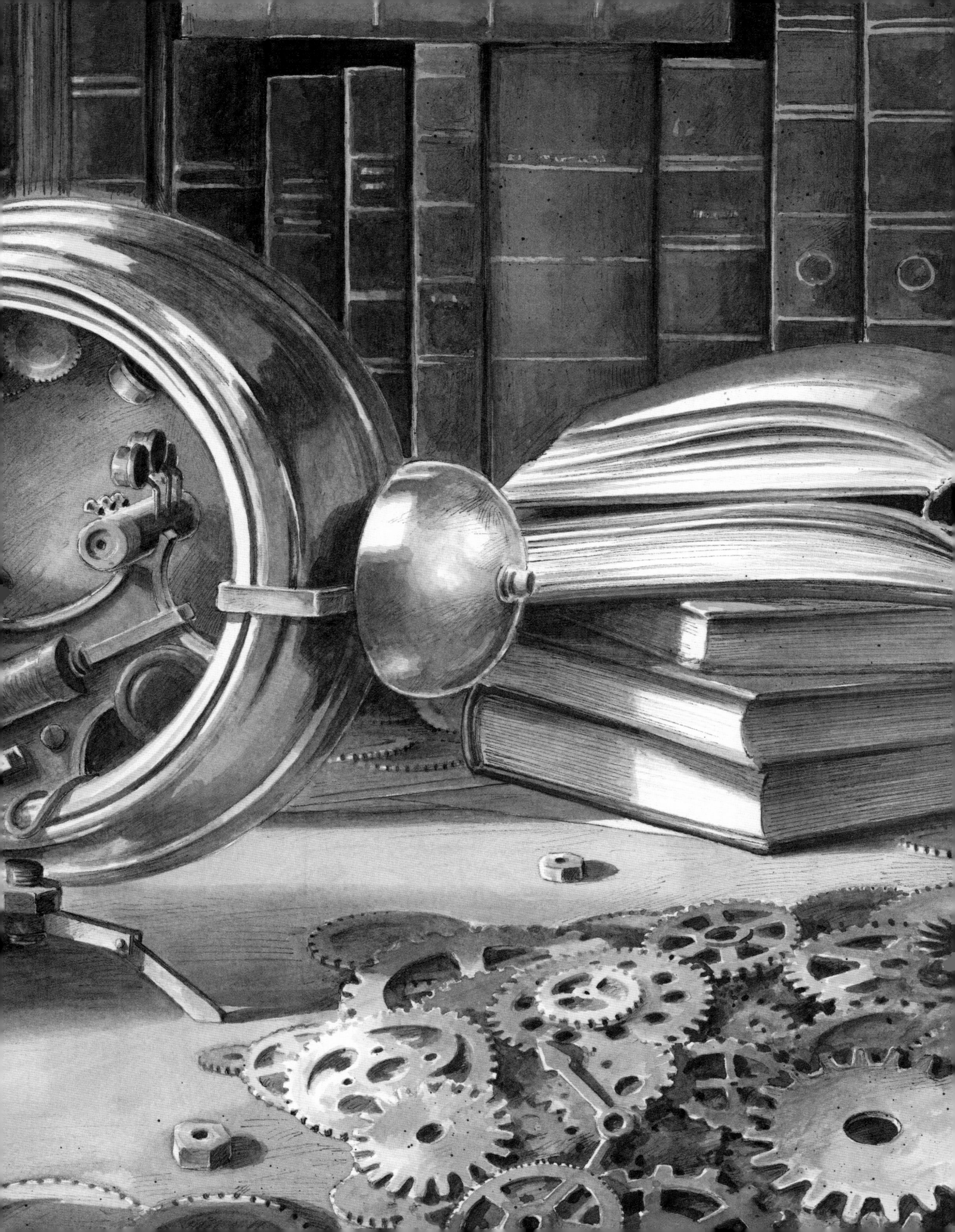

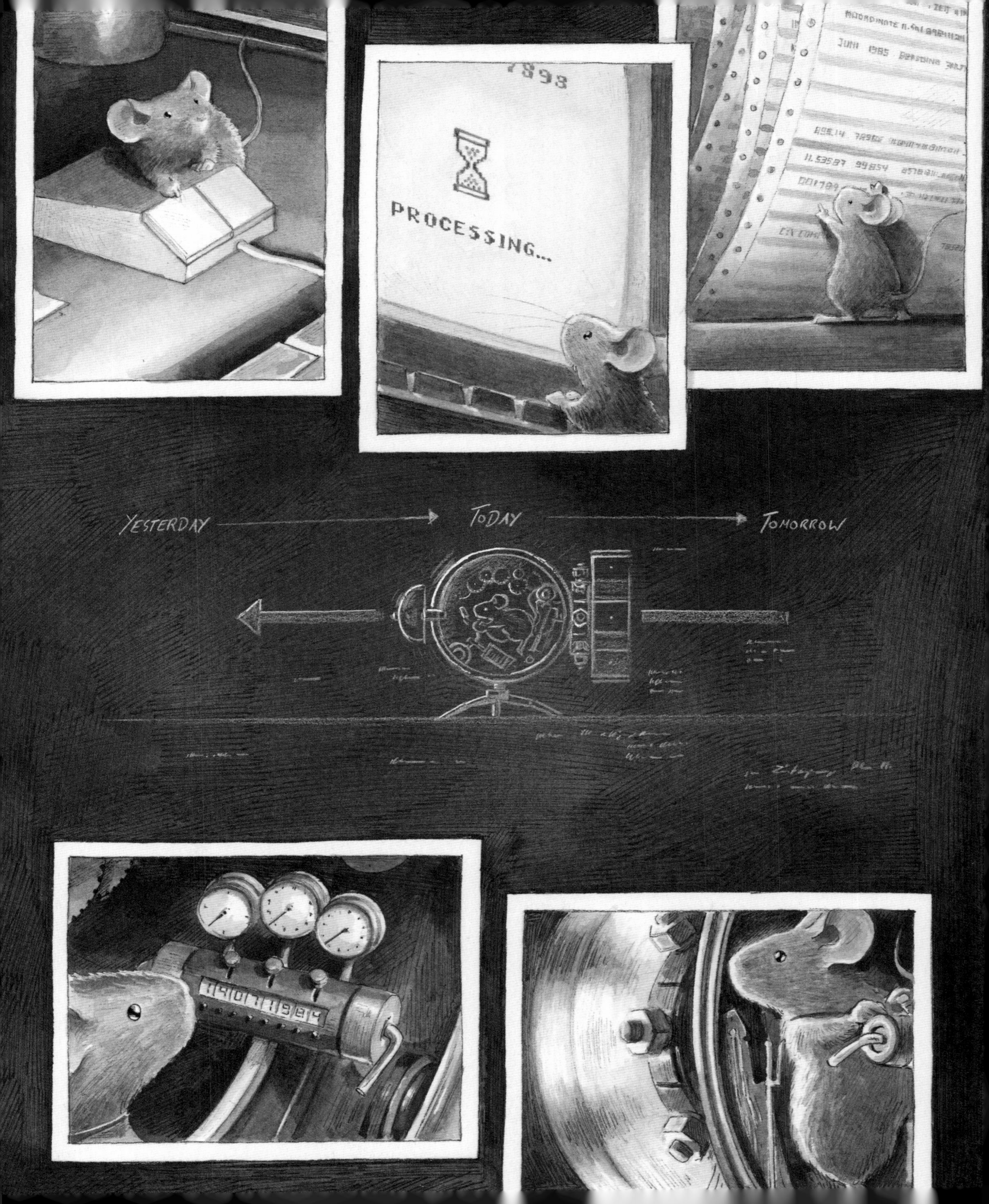
PROCESSING...
YESTERDAY
TODAY
TOMORROW

Back to the past

The time machine was ready. The original alarm clock was barely recognizable. Only the round brass casing was still clearly visible, but it was filled with all kinds of technical jumble. Meanwhile, the date for the launch back through time had been calculated. The calculations had been so complicated that the little mouse's brain simply couldn't reach a conclusion—even though fortunately it had recovered from the blow to the head. A computer, however, fed with vast quantities of figures, spat out the solution.

The mouse packed only the most necessary things. He stowed his notebook with all his calculations behind the seat, and of course he also took the clockmaker's pocket watch. He gazed at it once more with pride—the handicraft really was masterly.

The time machine's engine sprang to life. The solenoid coils began to rotate, and the whole machine began to vibrate. At first there was a muffled electric hum, but as the motor turned faster, so the sound rose higher and higher. Sparks began to fly from the now-glowing wires, followed by dazzling flashes. And then suddenly there was complete silence. The engine went on turning almost without a sound. And the little mouse inside the machine sensed that all around him things were changing.

With one more bright flash, the mouse and his time machine disappeared from the here and now.

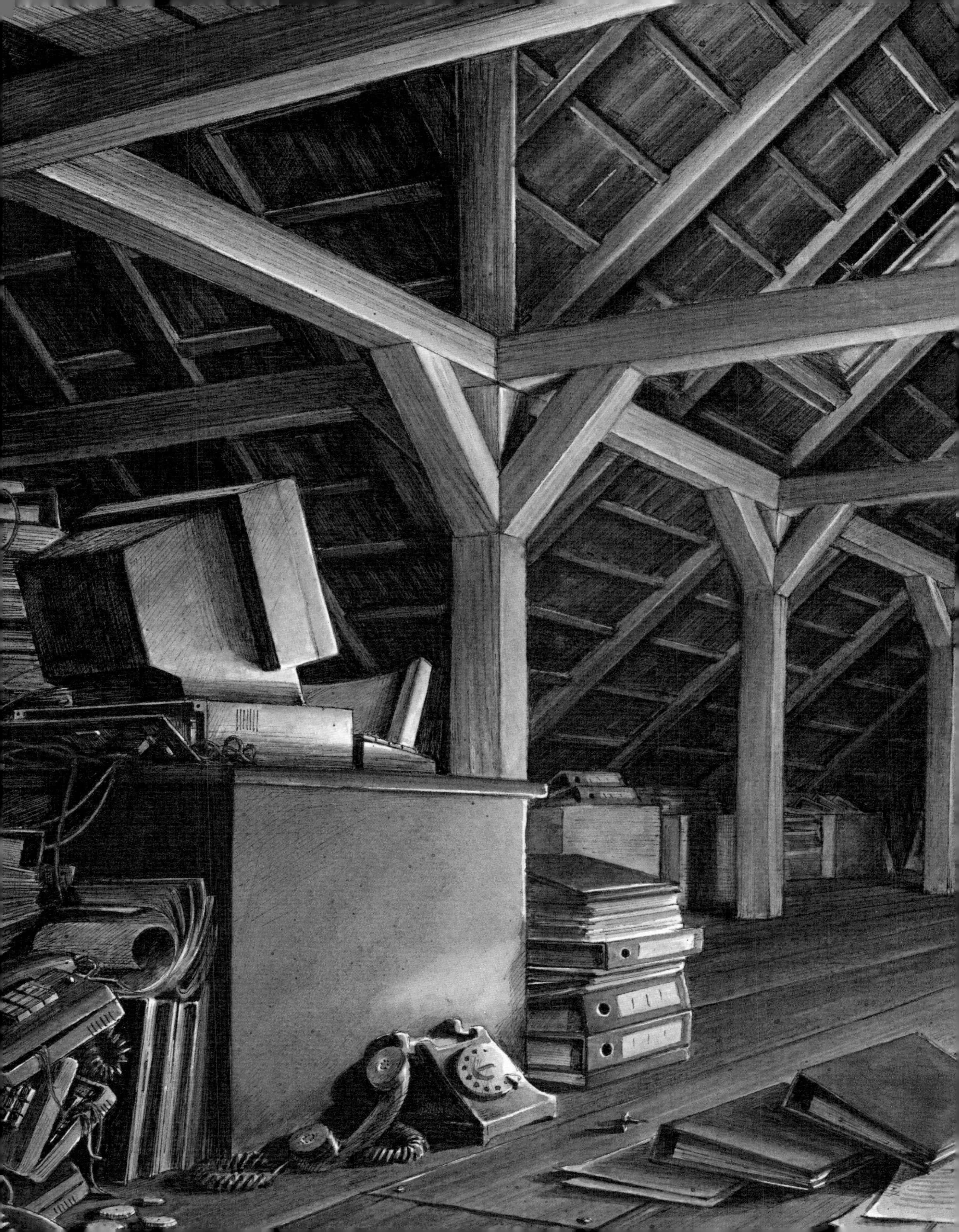

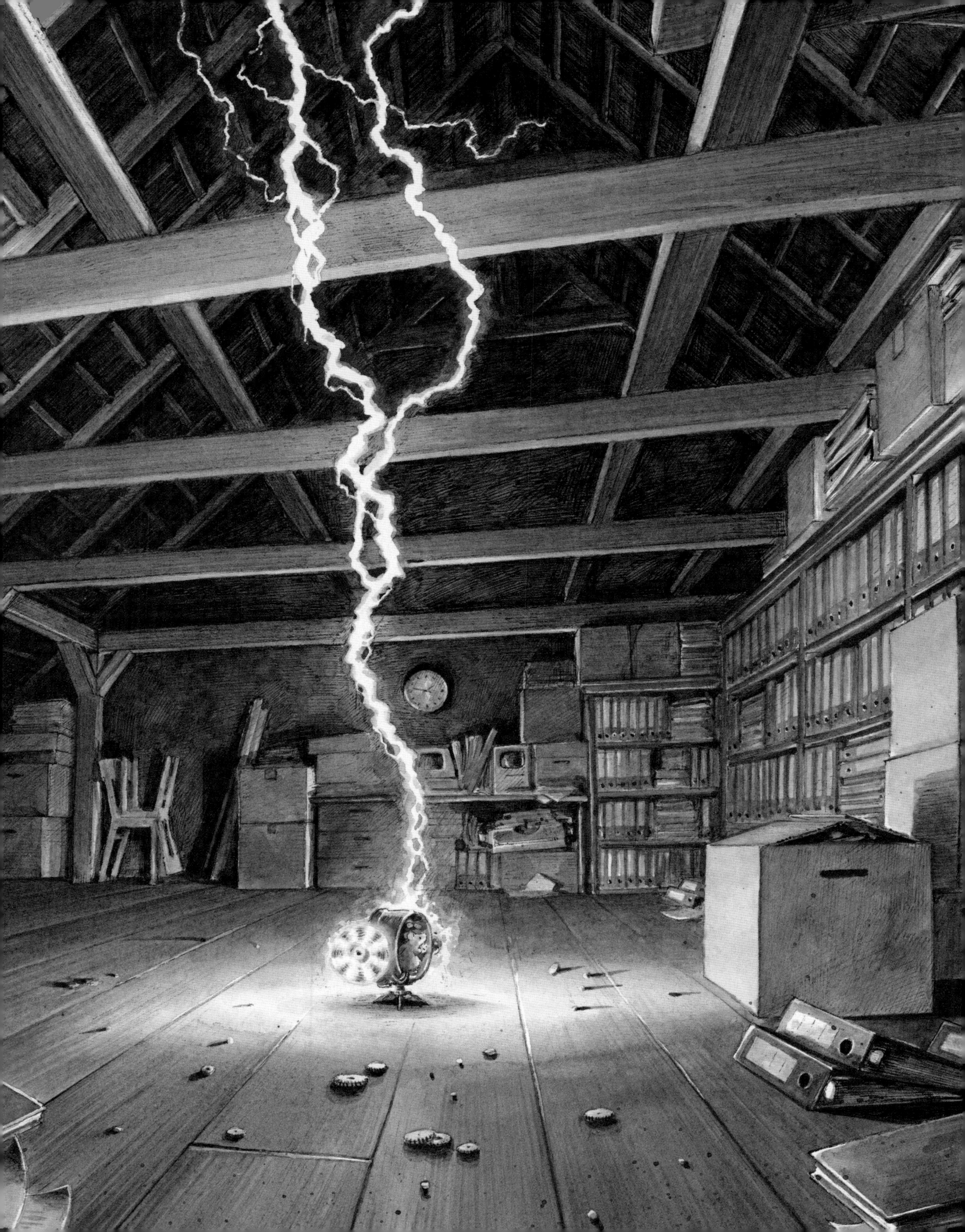

Was time really running backward? At first all that the little mouse could see was that the hands of a wall clock in one corner of the room had stopped, and then as if directed by some ghostly fingers, they started to move in a counterclockwise direction. Faster and faster.

Outside, a new day dawned. Or was it perhaps the day before? Yesterday? The sun appeared in the little window of the attic, but it too was moving in the wrong direction. Faster and faster it headed toward the east. There was a short twilight as the color of the sky changed from blue to pink to black. The short, starlit night was then followed by an even shorter day. The day before yesterday! This time the sun positively sprinted across the little window. Outside it went dark and then immediately light again.

Very soon the sun had ceased to be a circular disk and had become nothing but a passing streak of light. The hands of the wall clock were no longer even visible, as they were moving so fast around the clock face. The constant switch from day to night to day became a blur. The mouse was quite hypnotized by time racing backward; how far back had he gone? A few past moments flashed before him and answered his question. For a fraction of a second he could see himself. It was the time when he was trying to put the heavy book about Einstein's theories back on the shelf. Hadn't he seen a bolt of lightning then? . . .

With this thought, the shape of the attic around him became blurred, and the flickerings of day and night gave way to a steady gray. The time-traveling mouse had fallen out of time.

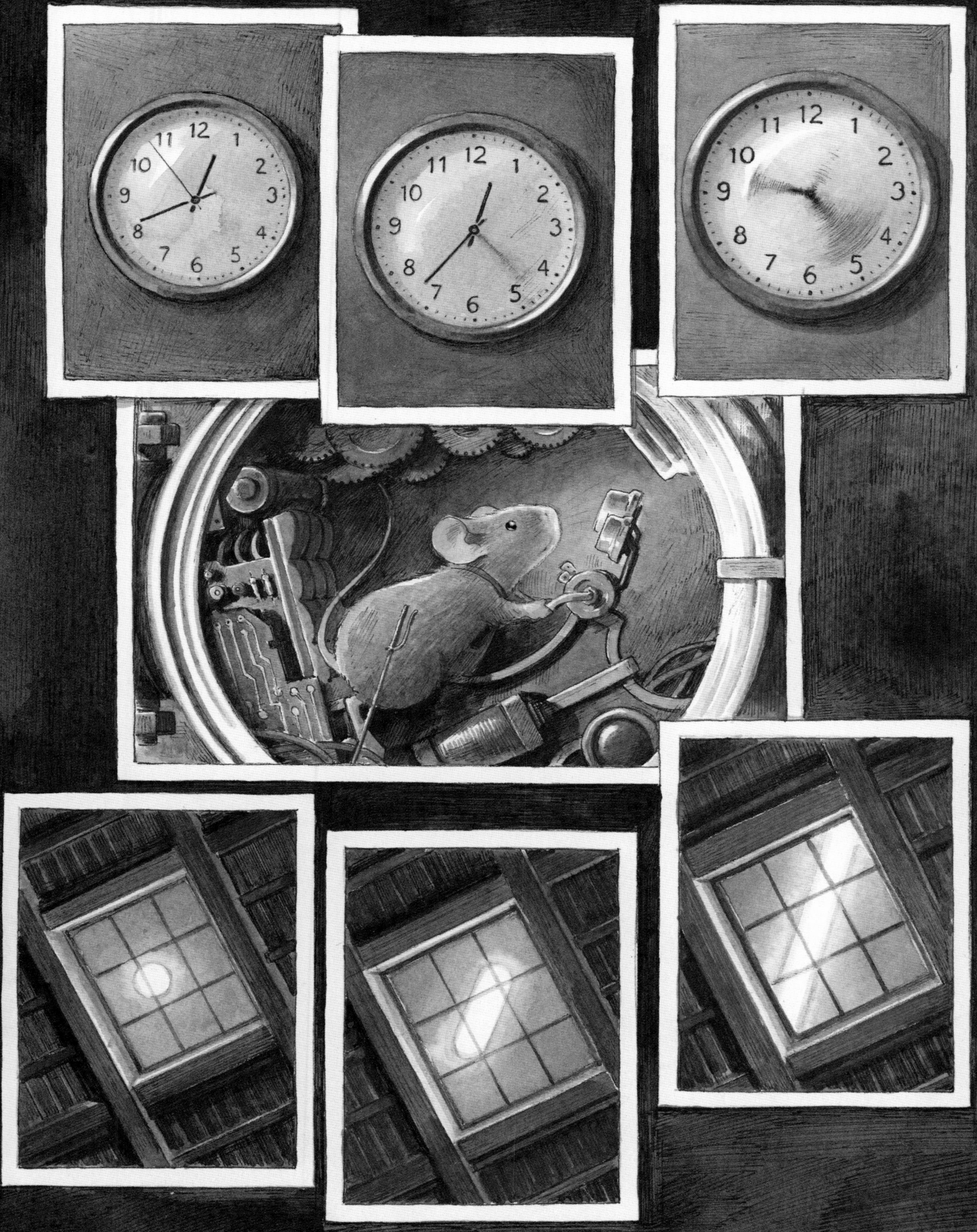

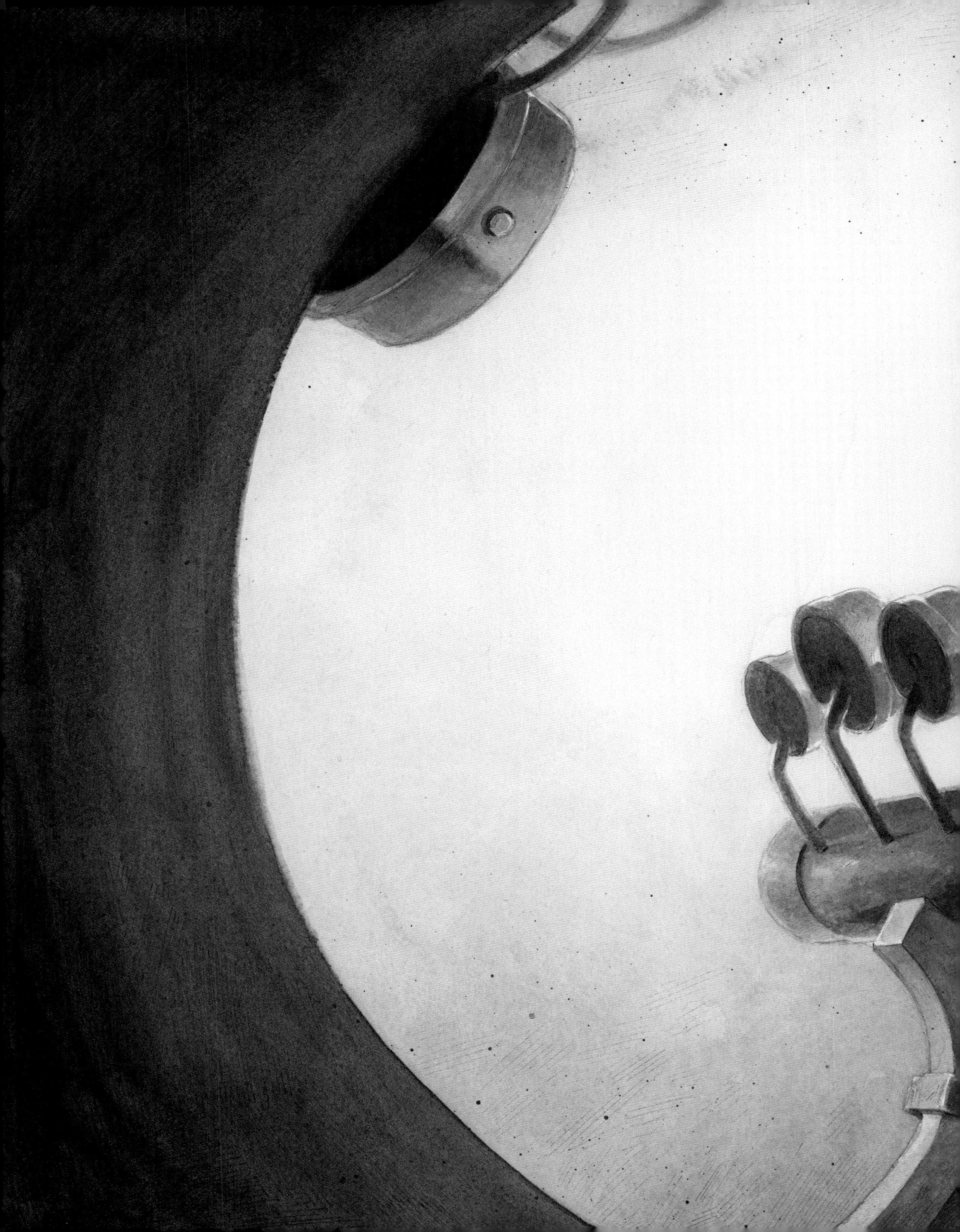

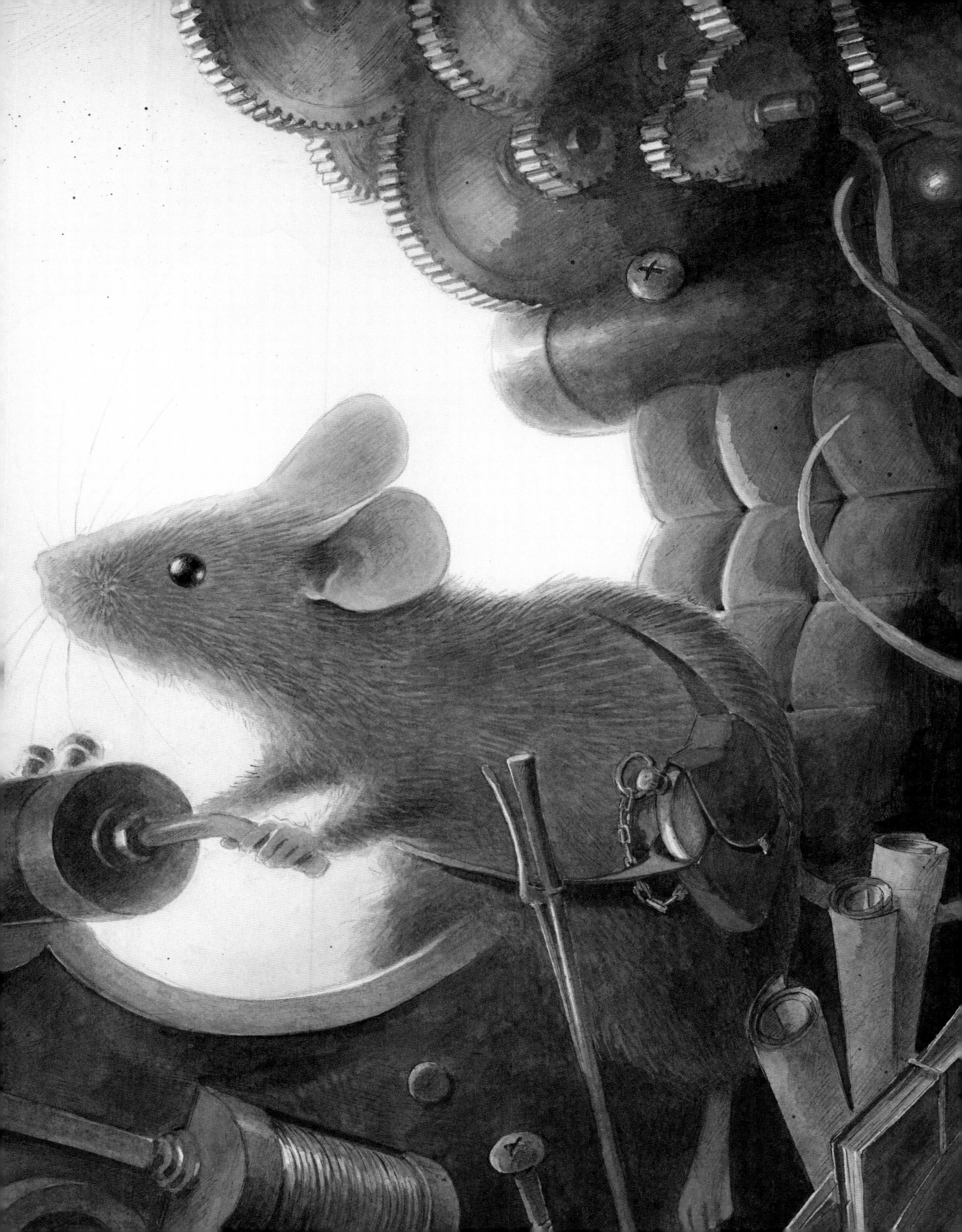

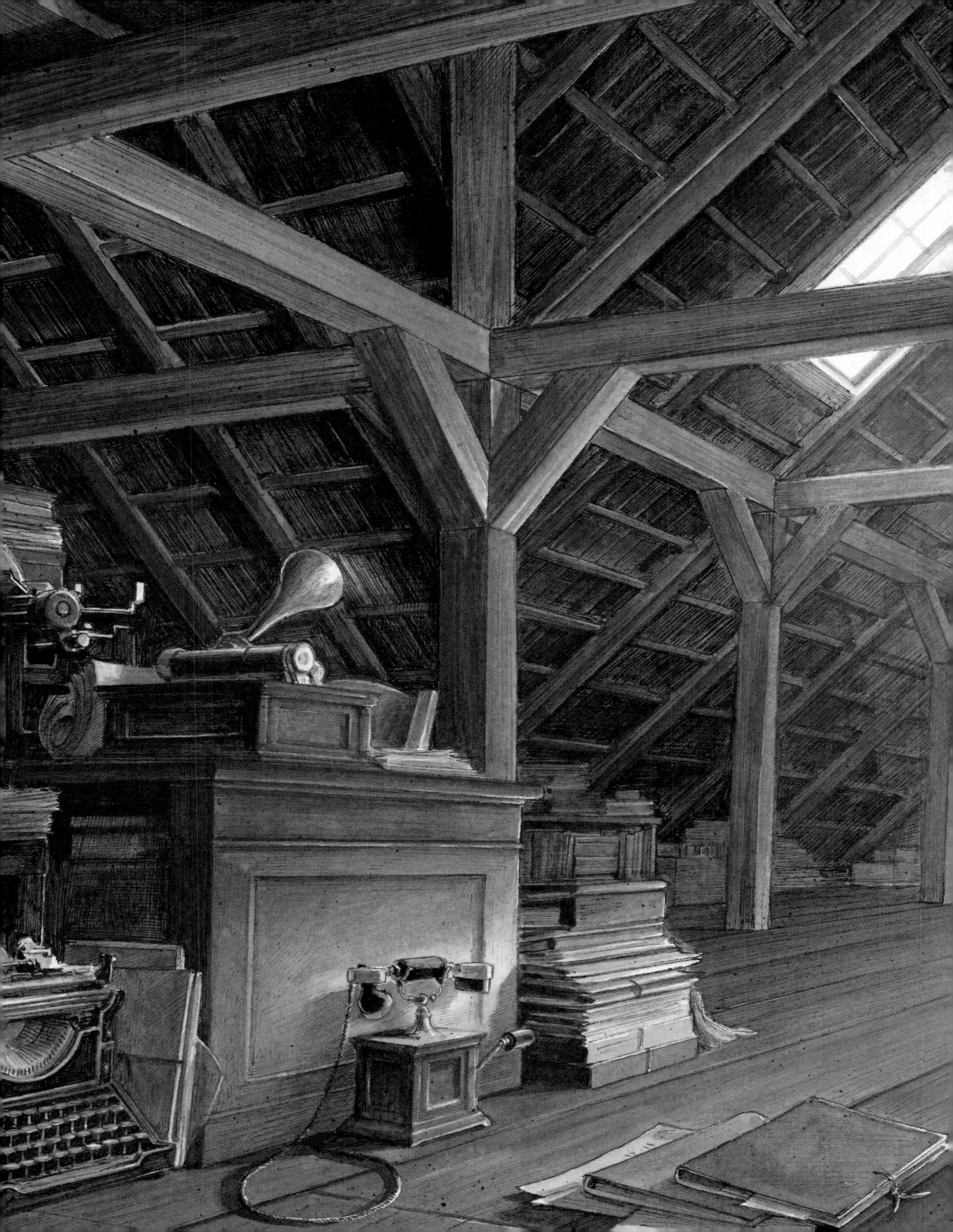

Suddenly the strange journey was over. The mouse found himself once more standing with his invention on the floorboards of the attic, high up in the Bernese patent office, almost as if nothing had happened. The time machine's engine had stopped. Some of the wires were still glowing and smoking. Had it really gone backward in time? Would he now be able to go to the cheese fair? He swiftly grabbed his pocket watch and set off on his way. He was so excited by the prospect of all that cheese that he hadn't noticed that everything around him in the attic had changed completely.

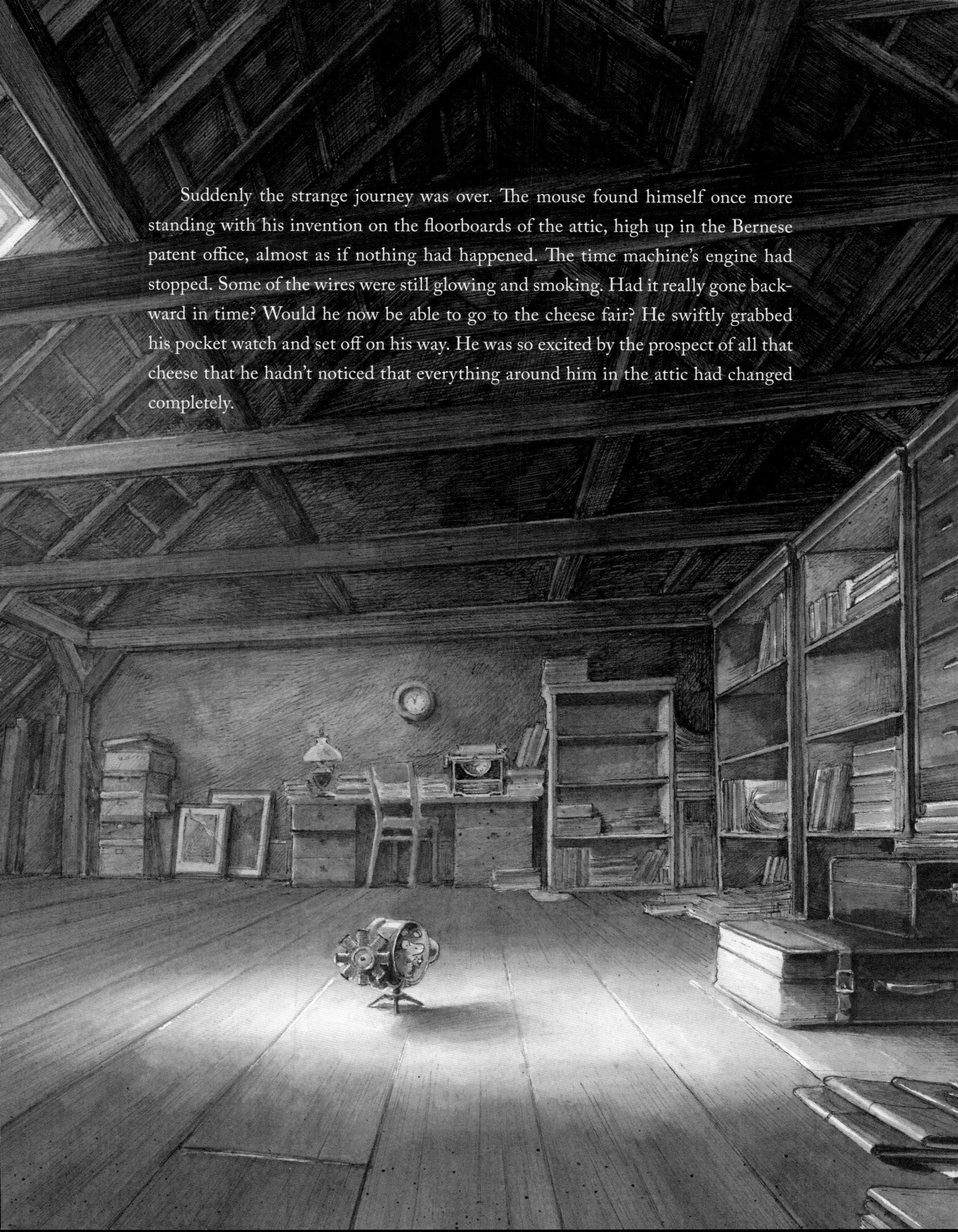

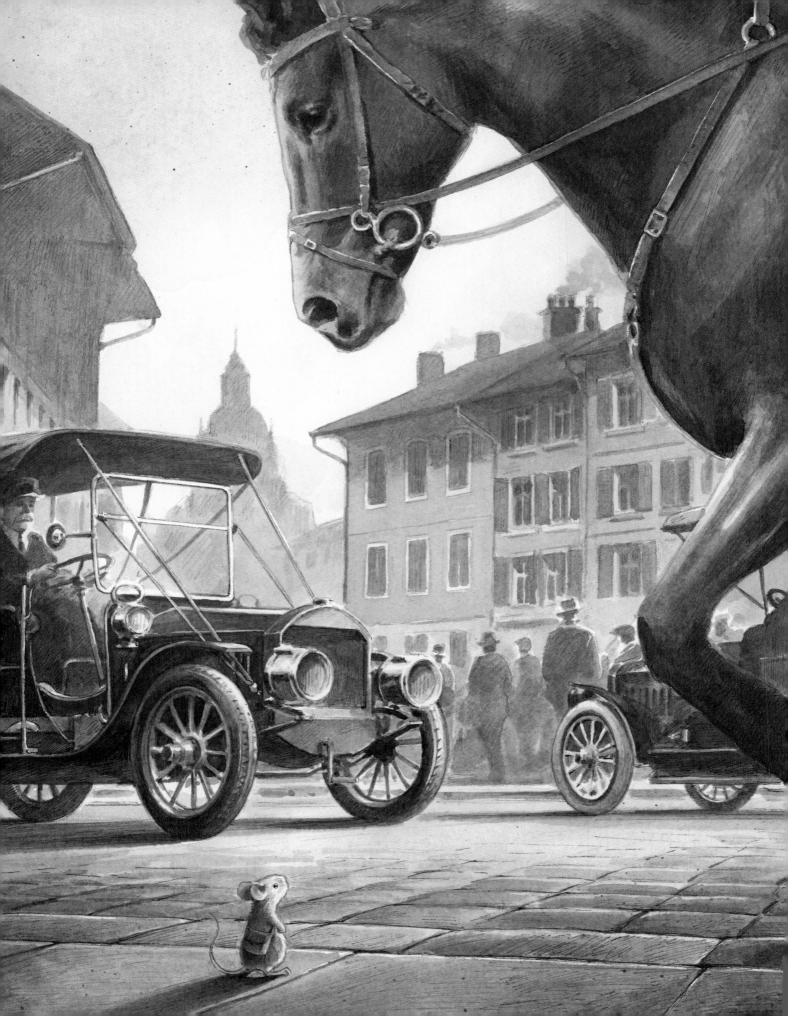

In a strange time

The little mouse stood wide-eyed in the street. Instead of the usual cars and buses there were now horse-drawn carriages rumbling over the rough cobblestones. He jumped at the sound of a honking horn. The sounds came from a passing car, but it looked just like one of the horse-drawn carriages with a smoking engine built into it. There were humans all around, but they were dressed in strange clothes. The women wore long dresses, and the men wore suits with jackets that seemed too wide for them. They were all wearing hats. Where on Earth had the little mouse landed? Or maybe the question should be, *when* had he landed?

Staying close to the gutter, he scurried anxiously through the streets. The gutter would protect him against people's shoes and horses' hooves. But he had no idea where he was heading. He simply hoped he would find someone who could answer his question. Then suddenly he found himself standing outside a familiar place.

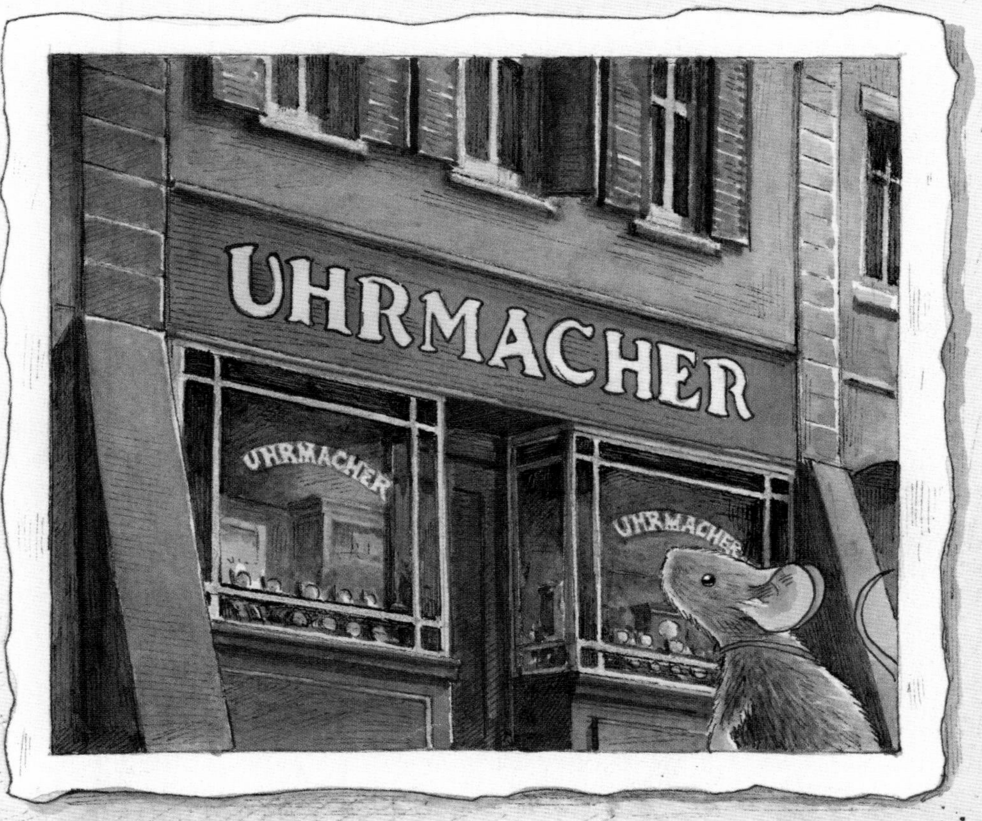
UHRMACHER
UHRMACHER
UHRMACHER

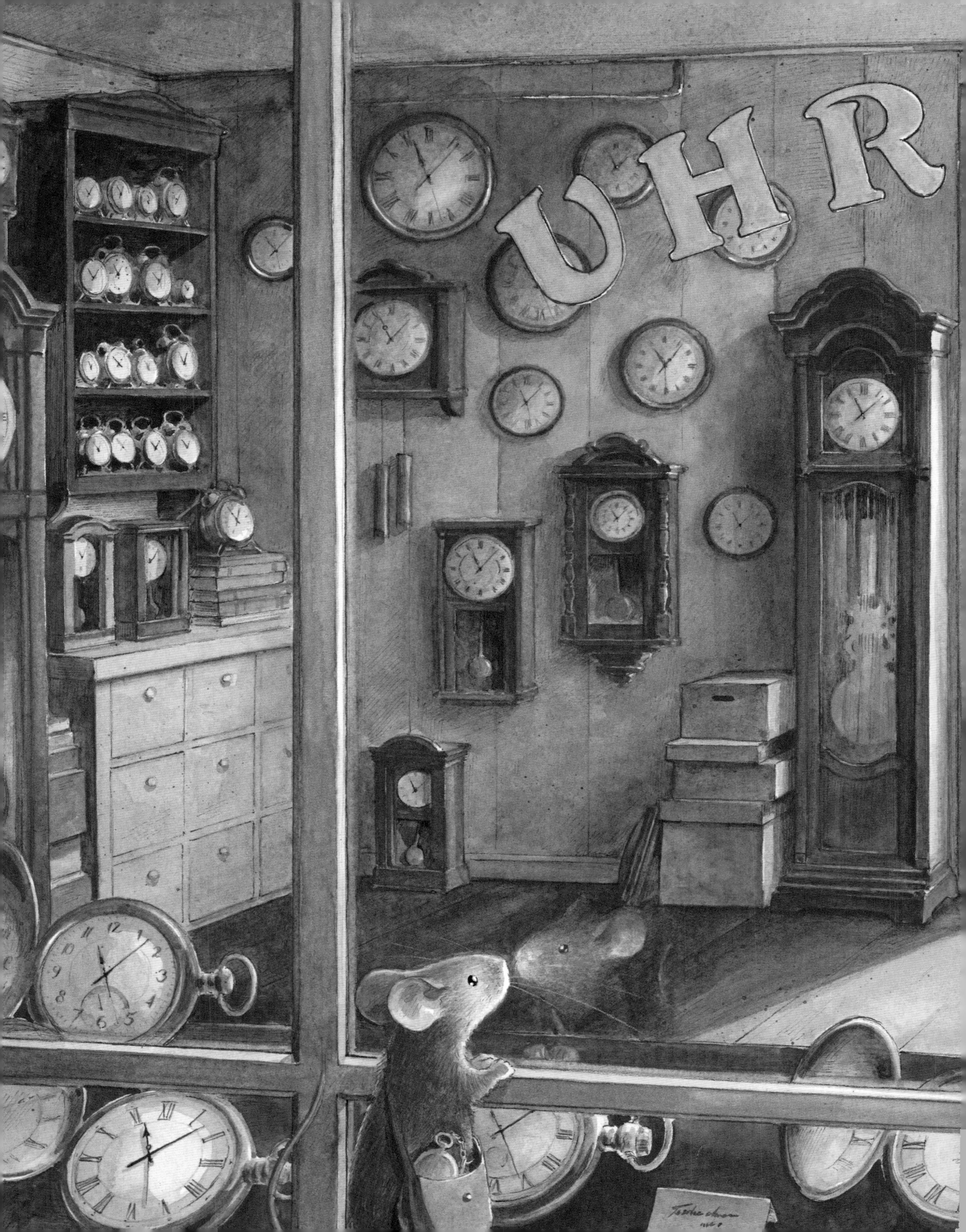
UHR

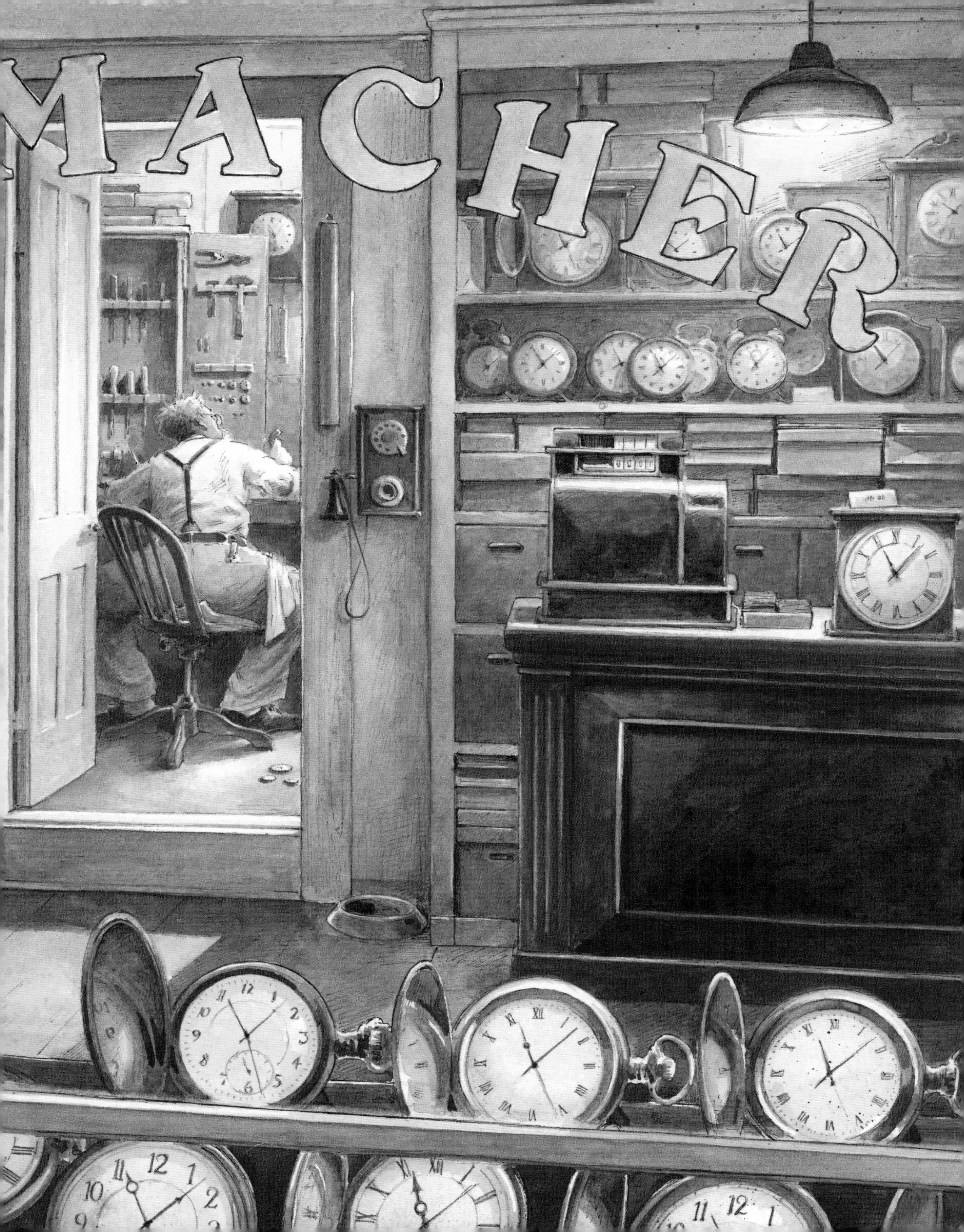
MACHER

By now it was darkest night. The little mouse had cautiously waited until the coast was clear. Now he hopped up onto the door handle and began to pull at it. He had no trouble cracking the lock, but it proved a lot harder to get the massive shop door to open. At last, however, there was a click and a quiet creak, and it opened just a tiny crack through which the little mouse was able to squeeze.

The shop was empty. There was no sign of the old man who had been working there just a short while ago. Just the constant ticking of countless clocks coming through the darkness.

The sounds of the shop hadn't changed at all—but everything else had. The little mouse used the opportunity offered by all the clocks around him to adjust his pocket watch, and then he cautiously made his way to the farthest corner. He hoped he would find the clockmaker's workshop there and get a few answers.

"Hello!" he shouted into the mouse hole, but the only answer was the echo of his own voice. He waited and stared into the darkness. Once more he called out. "Hello! I need your help!" His voice trembled slightly. But again there was no answer. No one was there.

Rather despairingly, the little mouse looked around. Were there no clues at all? A calendar or a newspaper with the date on it?

And then he discovered the feeding bowl.

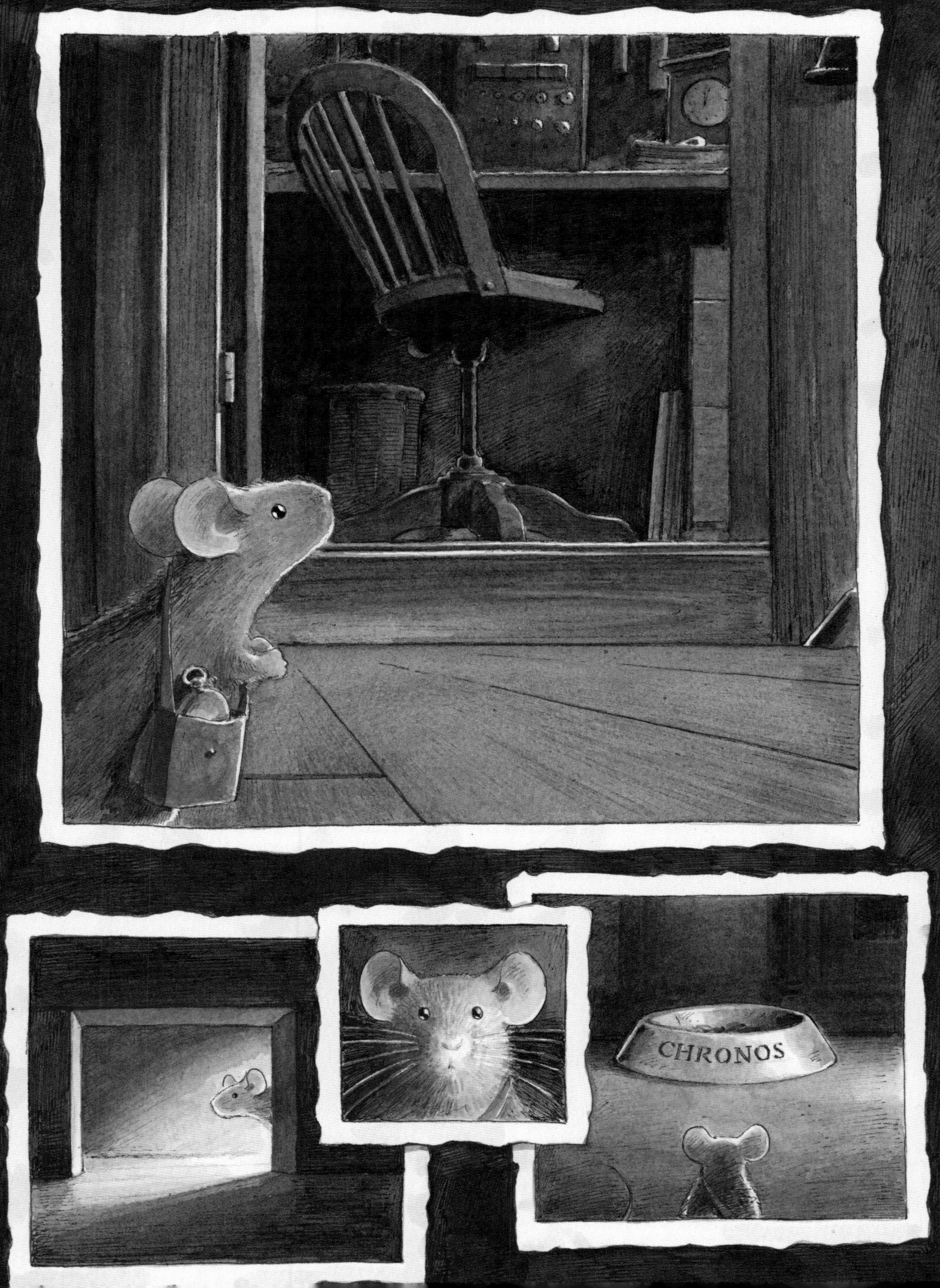
CHRONOS

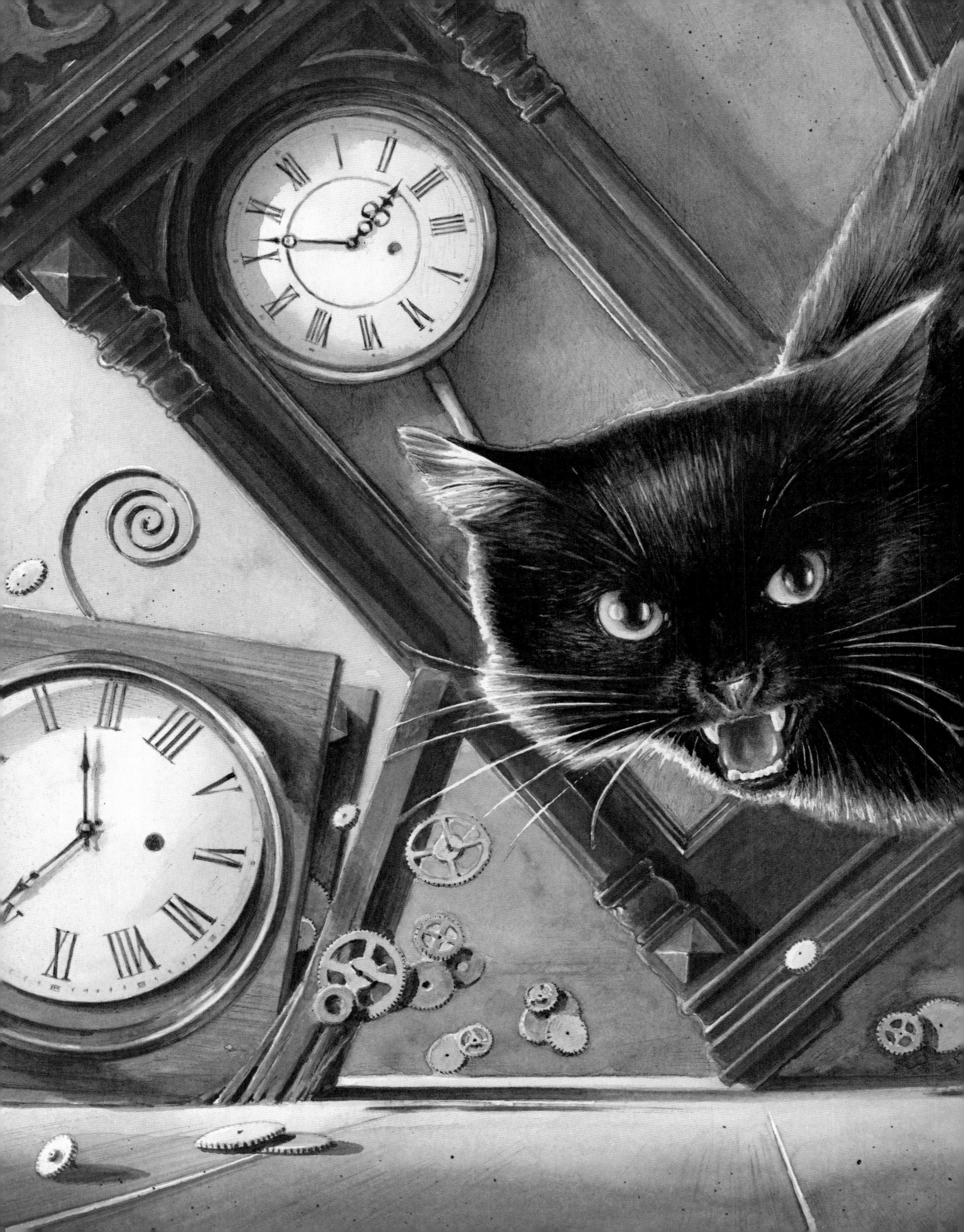

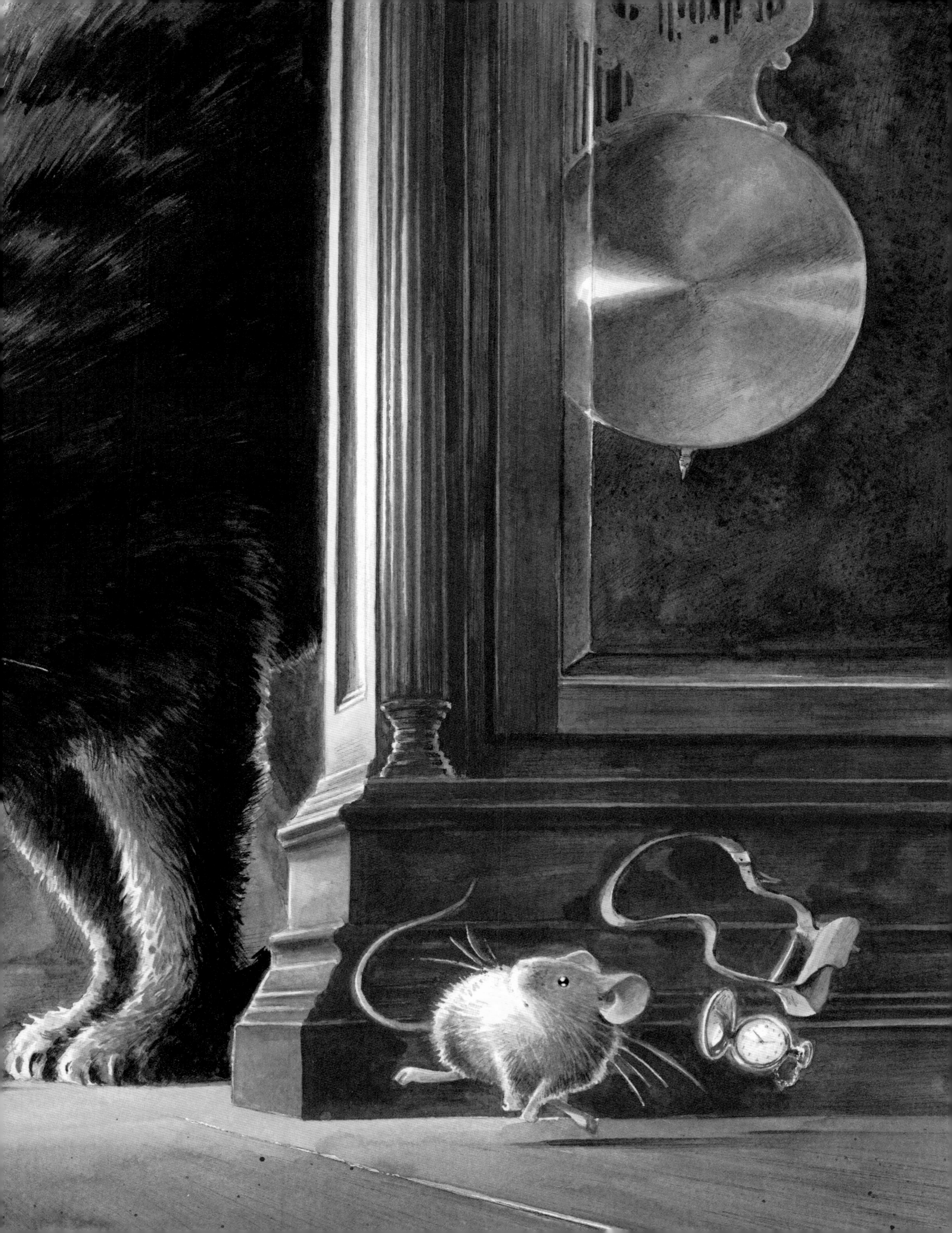

Chronos

Like a black shadow, the monster leaped out from behind a grandfather clock. His jaws were wide open, and he was hissing like a snake. So violent was his leap that he knocked over some of the clocks.

The little mouse jumped back in terror and stared as if in a trance at the terrible scene in front of him. It was almost as if time stood still for a moment. But then more clocks crashed to the floor and jerked him out of his shocked paralysis. Wooden frames split, panes of glass shattered, and cogwheels flew through the air.

The little mouse ran for his life. Only by a hair's breadth did he escape from the sharp claws, which dug into the floorboards instead of into his skin. The cat hissed again and came charging after the fleeing mouse with great leaps and bounds.

The mouse desperately looked for cover. He ran along the shelves and behind the grandfather clocks, but still he couldn't shake off his pursuer. Undeterred, the cat simply pushed every obstacle out of the way.

The mouse had just run around the big sales counter when his eyes fell on the shop door. It was still open just a crack. This was his chance. At top speed he hurtled through the gap. As soon as he had got through, he stepped to one side, huddled up against the wall, and held his breath. The cat somehow got through the gap as well and then went racing past. Swiftly the mouse went back through the crack and into the shop. With all his might he pushed the shop door until the latch finally clicked into place. He'd done it! He could still hear the hissing sound out in the street, but that quickly faded. And then the black shadow of Chronos the tomcat was swallowed up by the darkness of the night.

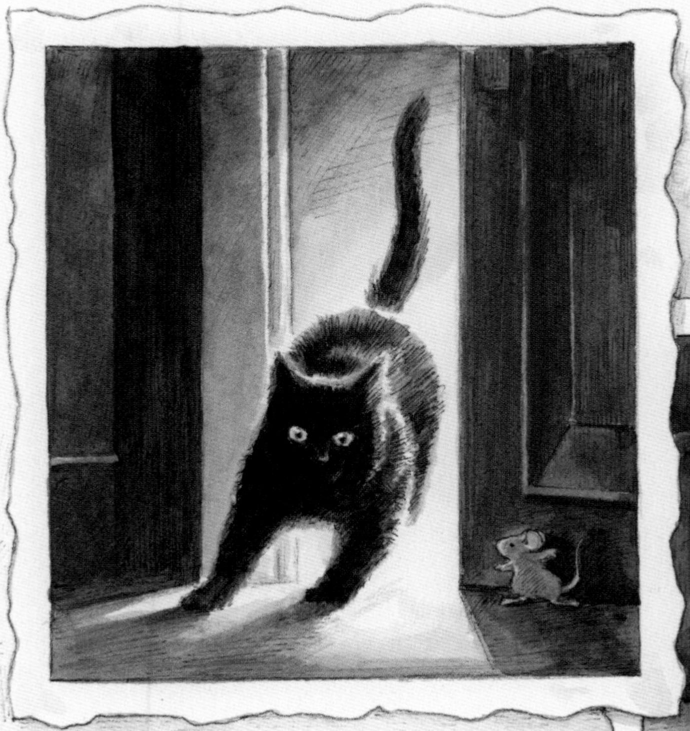

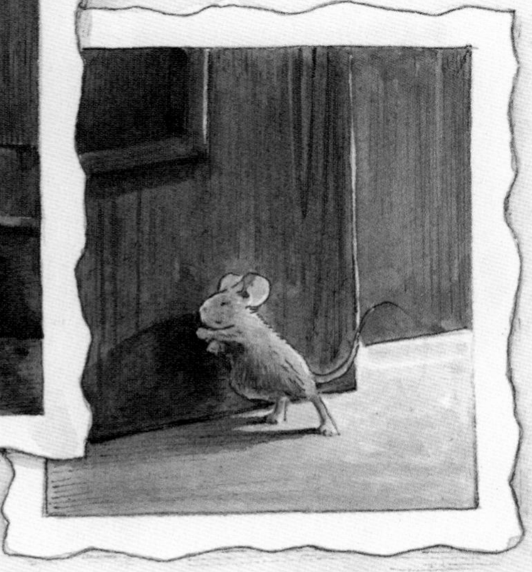

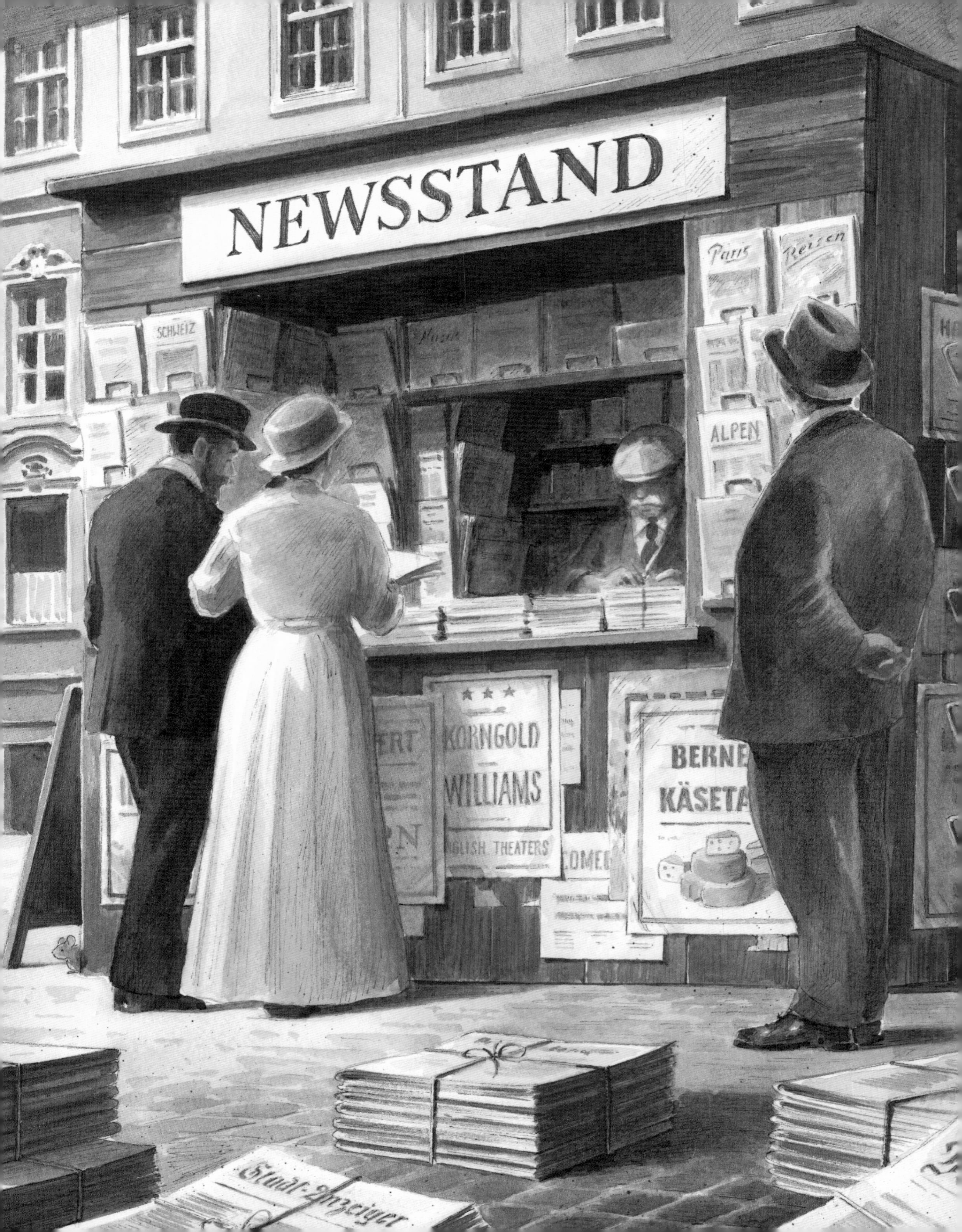
NEWSSTAND
SCHWEIZ
Paris
Reisen
ALPEN
KORNGOLD
WILLIAMS
BERNE
KÄSETA
Stadt-Anzeiger

Stranded

At the first light of dawn, the little mouse managed to pry the shop door open again and set out on his way. The encounter with the cat had given him a pretty good idea of the time in which he'd landed. But now he wanted to make certain. For a while he wandered through the empty streets until he came to a newspaper stand. It was still closed. But he listened to the conversation between some humans who were obviously also waiting for it to open.

"So when do the new papers arrive?" a thin man with a hat asked the vendor.

"Soon, probably around seven," the vendor replied as he unlocked his stand and started sorting the magazines.

"Seven?" murmured the little mouse, reaching into his pocket. That couldn't be far away. He wanted to check the time on his pocket watch; but only now did he remember that he'd put it in his shoulder bag, and he had left that behind.

A team of horses pulled up by the newspaper stand, and a young man wearing suspenders threw several bundles down on the pavement. When the vendor had finished sorting out all the different newspapers and the buyers had buried their noses in the freshly printed pages, the little mouse risked taking a peek himself. . . .

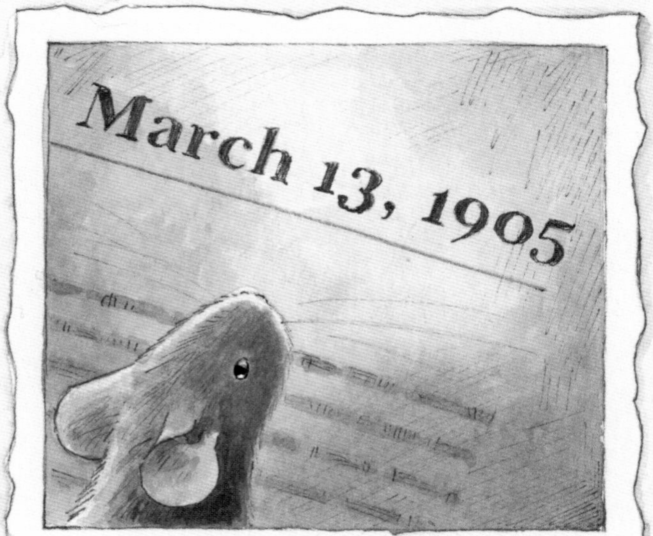
March 13, 1905

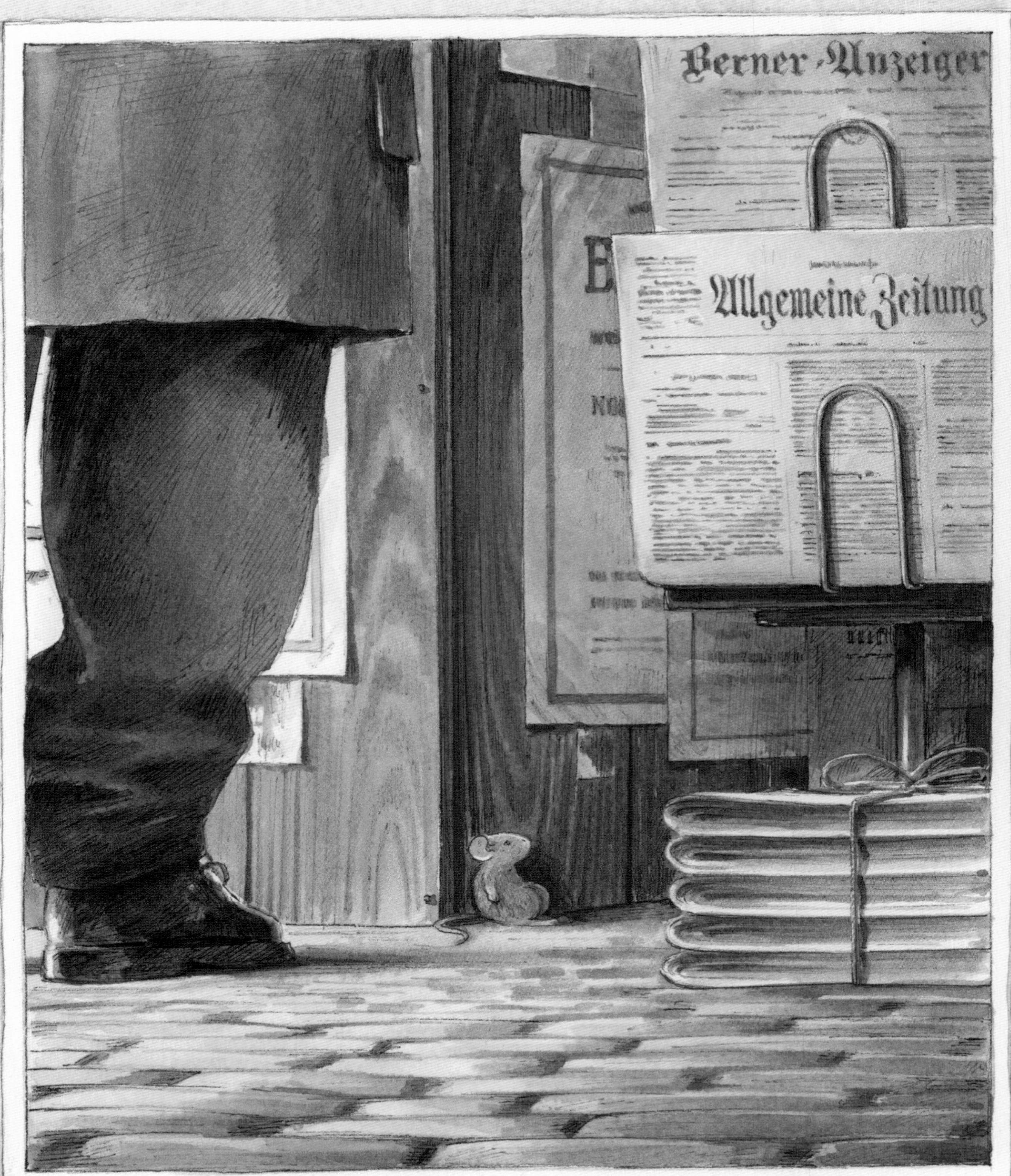
Berner-Anzeiger
Allgemeine Zeitung

On one of the papers displayed at the bottom of the stand he could clearly see a date. 1905. When he saw it printed there in black and white he gasped. He had missed his target by a good eighty years. Something must have gone wrong with his calculations. And if he could make one mistake, then the next journey could whisk him even further back into the past or even into the future. He would have to go through all his figures again and test all his formulas relating to space and time. He was still racking his brain when suddenly a look of panic covered his face and his heart began to thump. He had needed a computer in order to work out the coordinates for his time machine. But now he was stranded in a time when computers did not even exist. They would not exist for many, many years to come. The best he could hope for here was an adding machine. The little mouse drooped in utter despair. He would probably never be able to get back to his own time. And the cheese fair never even entered his mind.

Close to tears, he stared at the date again. 1905. And all at once a spark of hope lit up his black eyes. Maybe there was someone living at this time who could help him. And as if the universe had somehow arranged a miraculous coincidence, among the crowd of people now hurrying to work he spotted the very man.

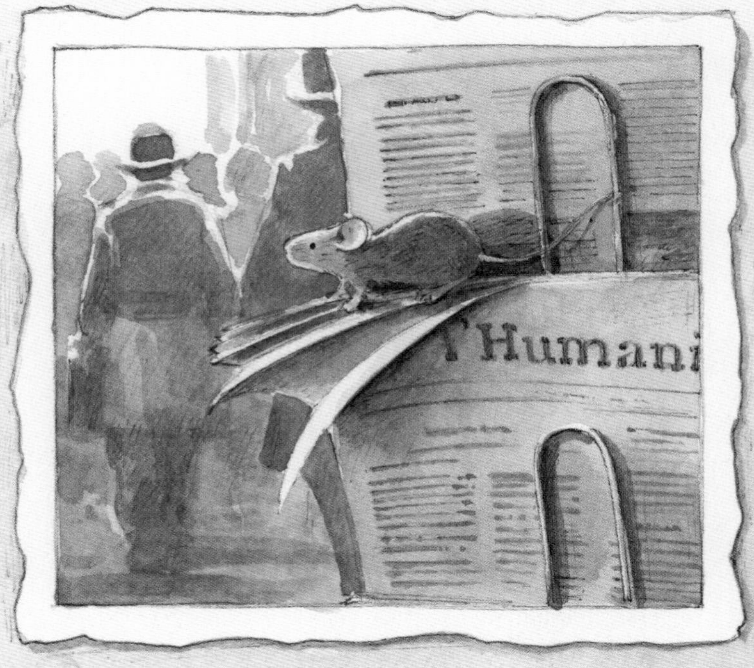
Humani

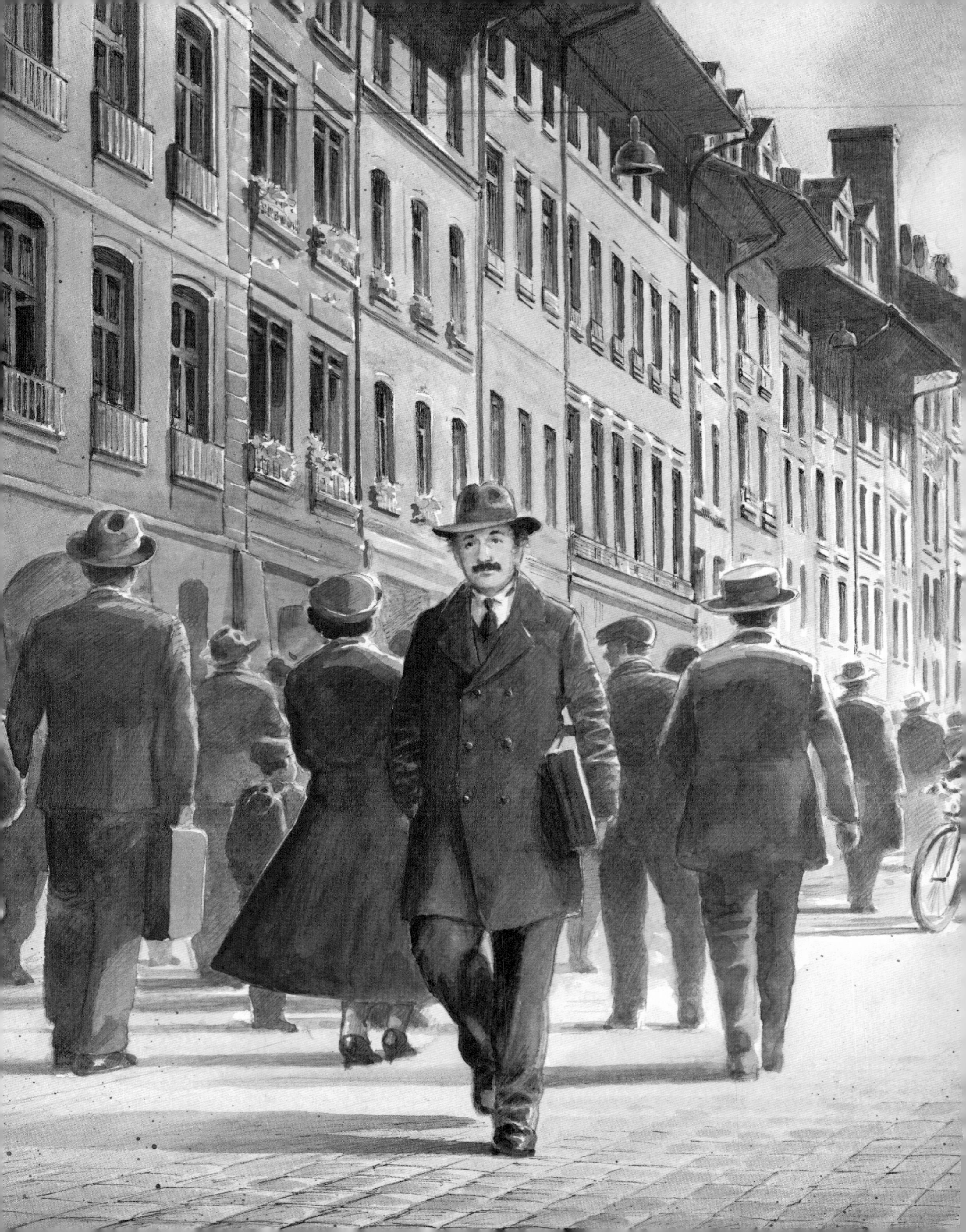

Allgemeine Zeitung
Neue Zürcher Zeitung
BERNER ANZEIGER
l'Humanité
Gazette de Lausanne

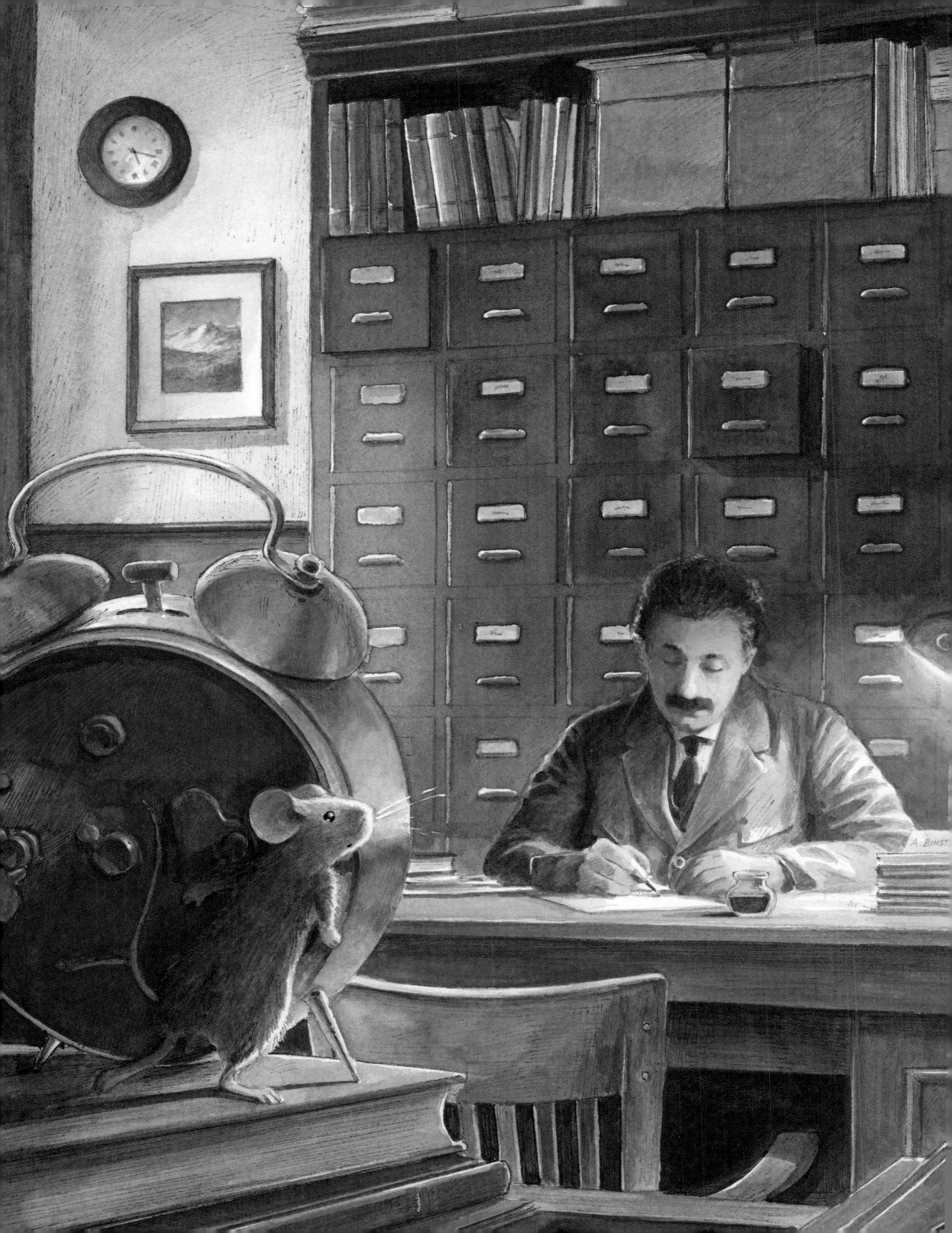
A. EINST

Einstein

The mouse followed him and watched as he sat at a desk that was much too small, bending over files and formulas. He was young—much younger than he was in most of the photographs that the little mouse had seen. But he already had his characteristic bushy mustache. His hair showed the first signs of what later became a tousled mane. Albert Einstein—the legendary scientist and Nobel Prize winner. But here he was now, just an ordinary employee working at the patent office.

It was Einstein's theories that had first paved the way for the little mouse's adventure. They had shown him an image of the world in which everything, including time, was relative. Would one of the most brilliant minds in human history perhaps be willing and able to help a little mouse who had fallen out of time?

For a few days the little mouse kept watch on Albert Einstein. Every day the great man would sit at his desk, stamp applications, and scribble a few comments. At lunchtime he would eat a sandwich he'd brought with him, and early in the evening he would switch off the light and leave the patent office. The little time traveler kept racking his brain. How could a mouse ask a human a question? And how could he do it without revealing the fact that the questioner was a mouse?

Then one evening when Einstein had gone home, the solution suddenly came to the little mouse. Einstein was a scientist, and scientists by their very nature were curious people. Maybe the little mouse could get him to play some kind of game. He picked up a fountain pen and began to write on a blank sheet of paper. He made the letters as big as he could so that they would look as if they'd been written by a human.

> *Dear Mr. Einstein,*
> *Would you please do me the honor of solving a riddle?*

Now he looked for a question that would be really easy to answer. But the last sentence should make Einstein curious.

> *On days when nothing's to be done,*
> *Who is often killed for fun?*
> *Who flies and yet stands still as well,*
> *Waits for no man but will tell?*
> *Turns night to day and day to night*
> *And yet bows down before the light?*

He laid the sheet of paper very visibly right in the middle of Einstein's desk.

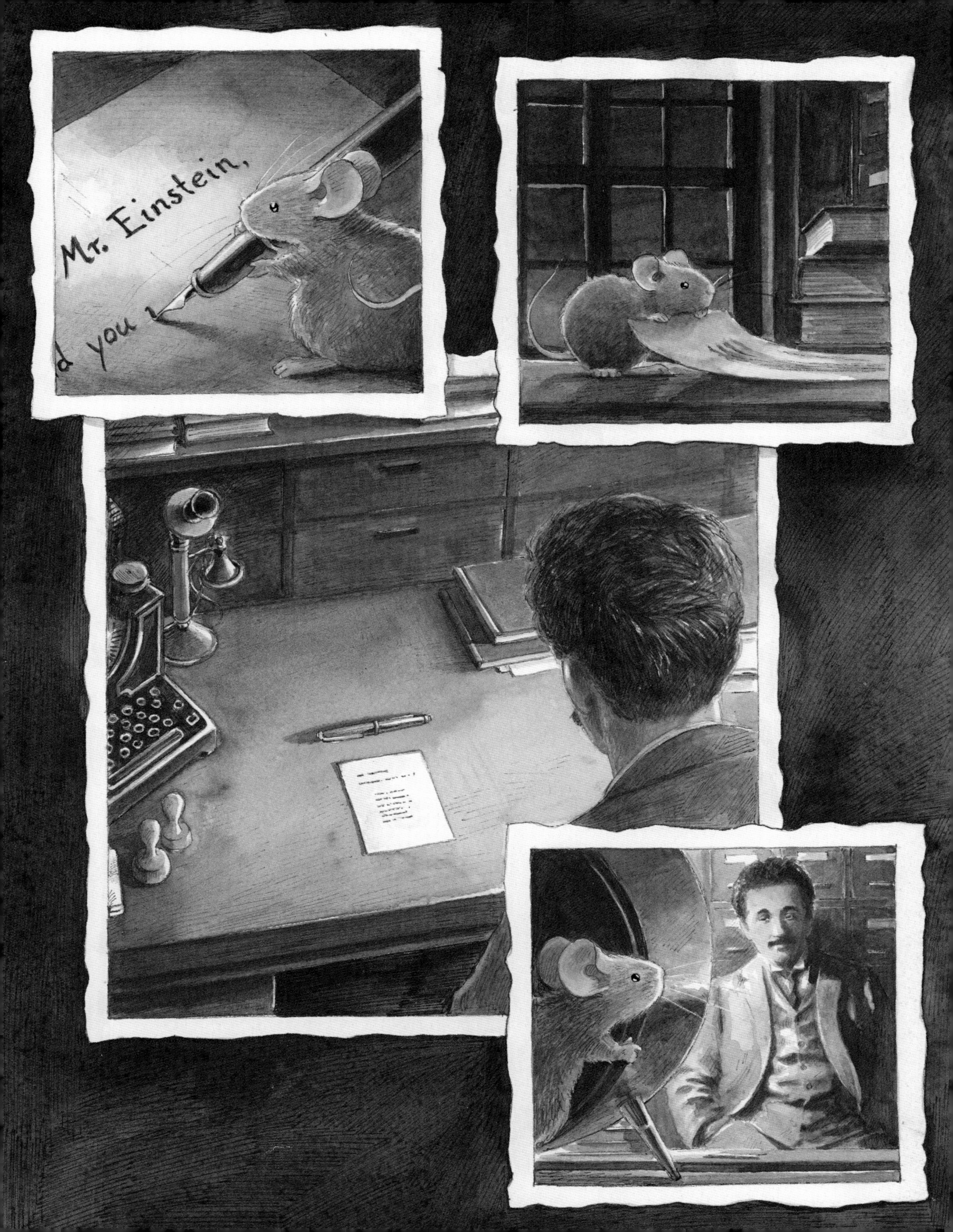
Mr. Einstein,
d you

The following evening the paper was still lying on the desk, but underneath the riddle was the handwritten answer:

> *Time!*
> *Yours respectfully,*
> *A. Einstein*

It had worked! This was the period in which Einstein must already have been formulating his first ideas about space and time—the little mouse was sure of that. And soon he would put together his famous theory of relativity, in which light was to play such an important role. It had been a good idea to relate time to light in the riddle. This must have aroused Einstein's interest.

Every evening now the little mouse left a riddle on the desk. Each one contained an increasingly complex mathematical query as well as equations about space and time. After a few days the stack of files on the desk had grown visibly higher. Einstein was spending most of the day trying to solve these ever more demanding riddles. It meant that his own work was now taking second place.

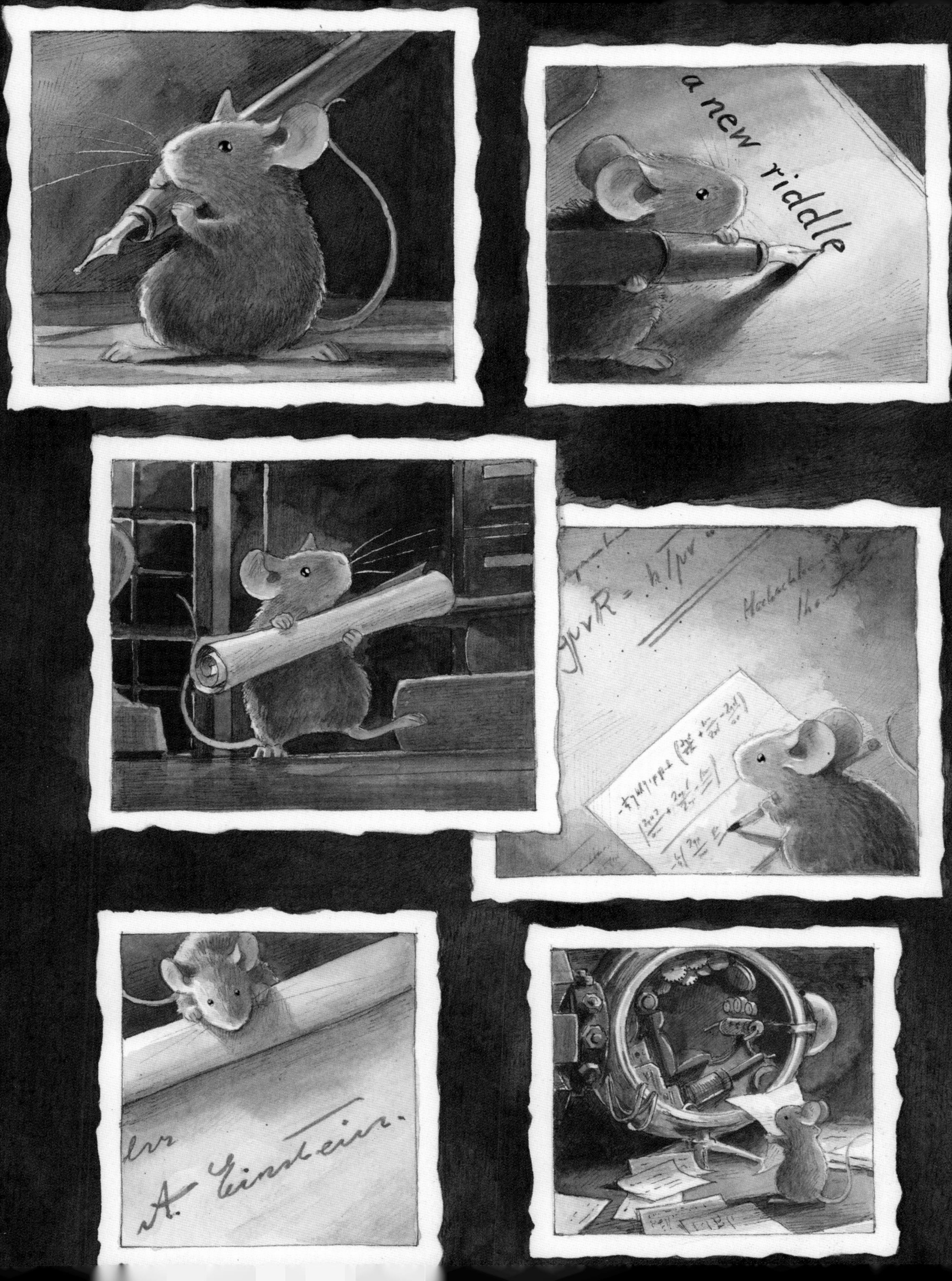
a new riddle
A. Einstein

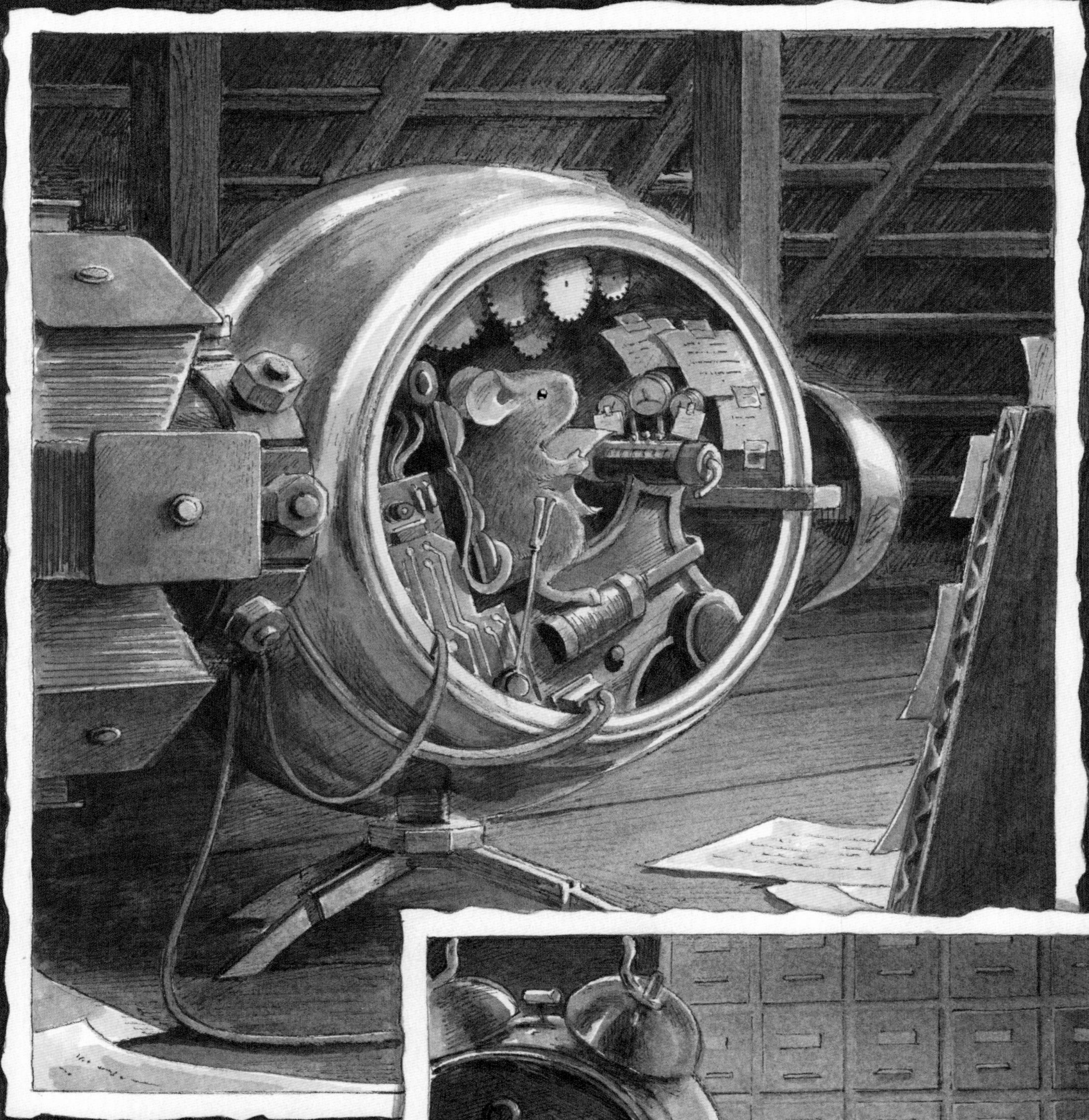
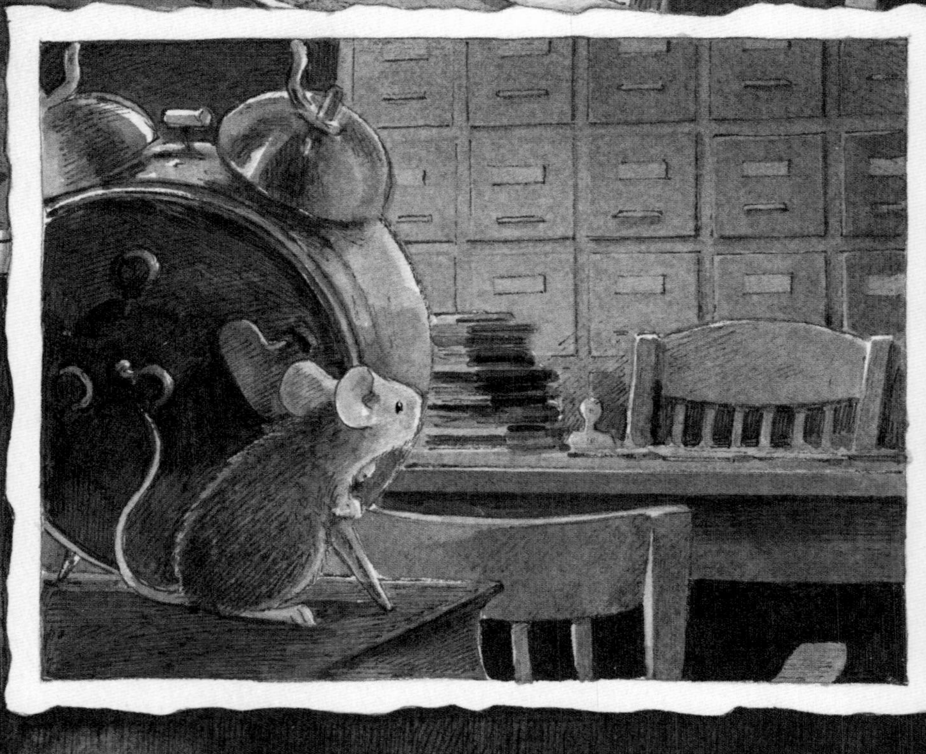

Tricked

He'd done it! The little mouse had collected Einstein's final answers. He was very excited, because now he had all the necessary facts and figures. He was so happy that he never even noticed that Einstein's desk was particularly full today.

Armed with the new calculations, the little mouse began to adjust his time machine, taking great care to ensure that a new journey would at last take him where—or rather when—he wanted to go to. He packed his notebook with all the calculations into the capsule. And once more he sadly remembered his lost pocket watch.

Finally, he picked up the last pieces of paper from the floor of the attic. Then suddenly he heard a noise. It was the creaking of wood. No question . . . someone was climbing the narrow wooden staircase that led to the attic. He looked fearfully in the direction from which the footsteps were growing ever nearer. And only now did he notice the footprints: a complete line of black marks on the wooden floorboards from one side of the room to the other. Panic-stricken, he looked down and saw the black soles of his own feet.

"Stamping ink!" murmured the mouse. What did it mean? The ever-louder footsteps forced him to concentrate again. At lightning speed, he made the final adjustments, packed as many papers as he could into the time machine, and started the engine. The wires had already begun to glow when the door to the attic sprang open.

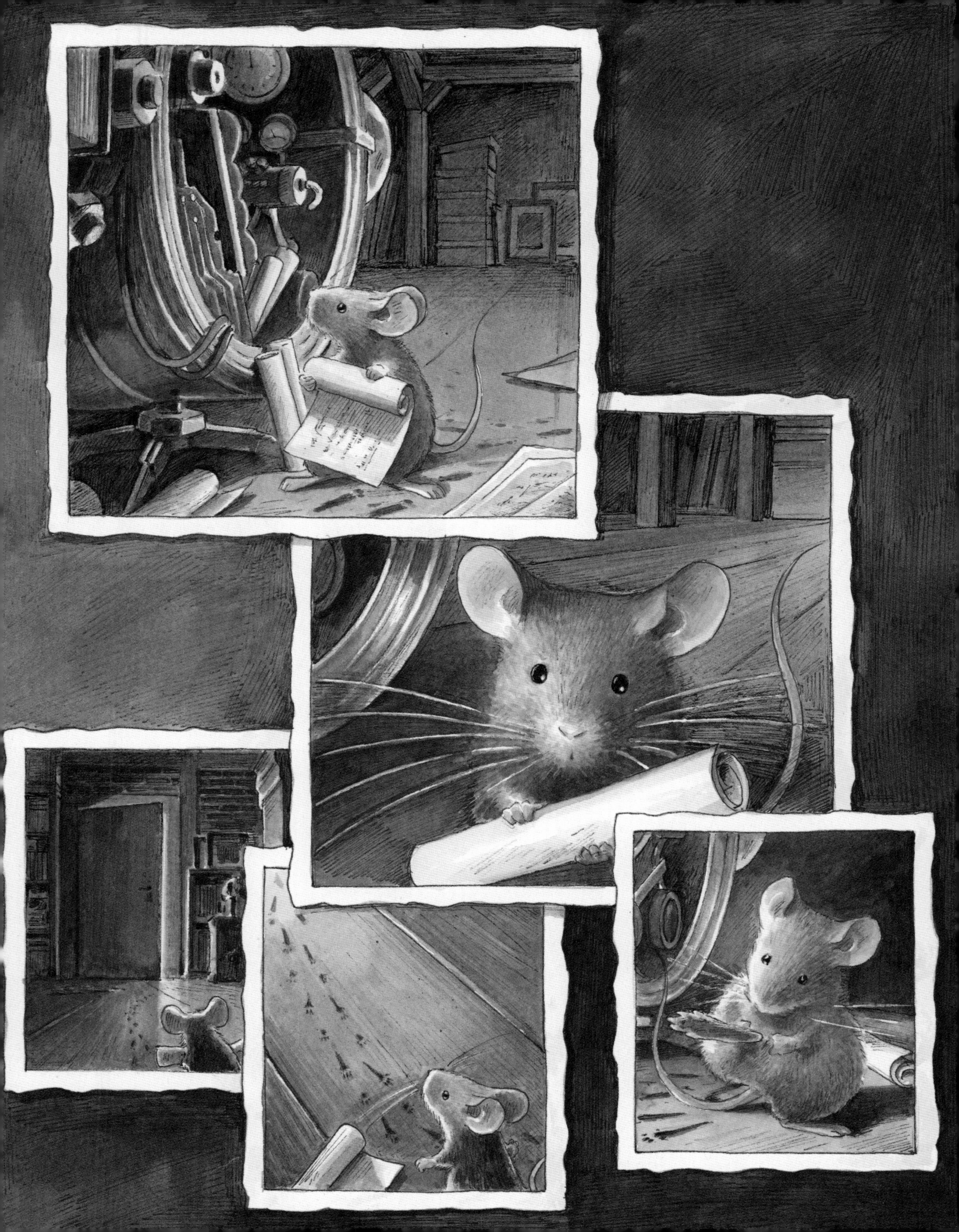

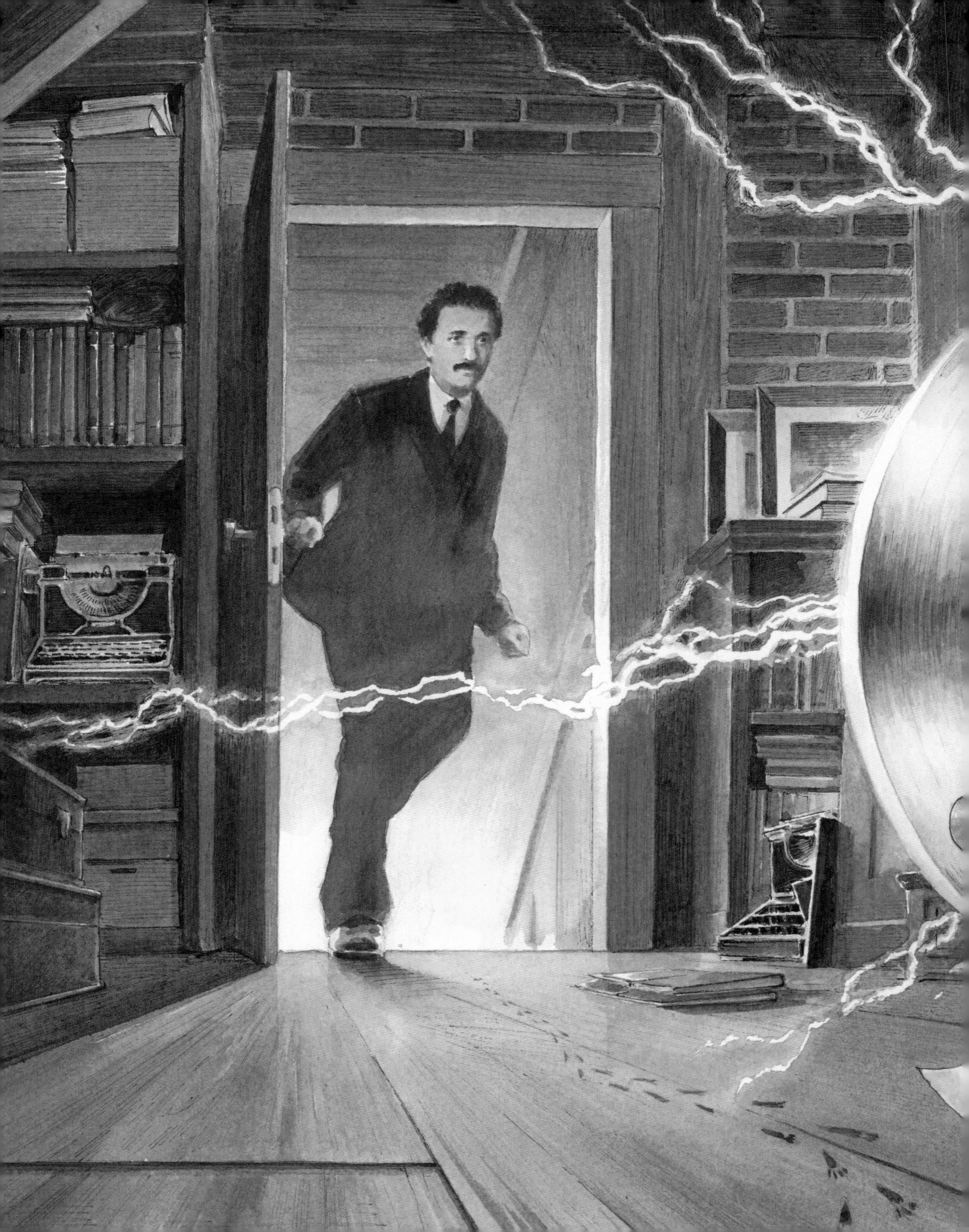

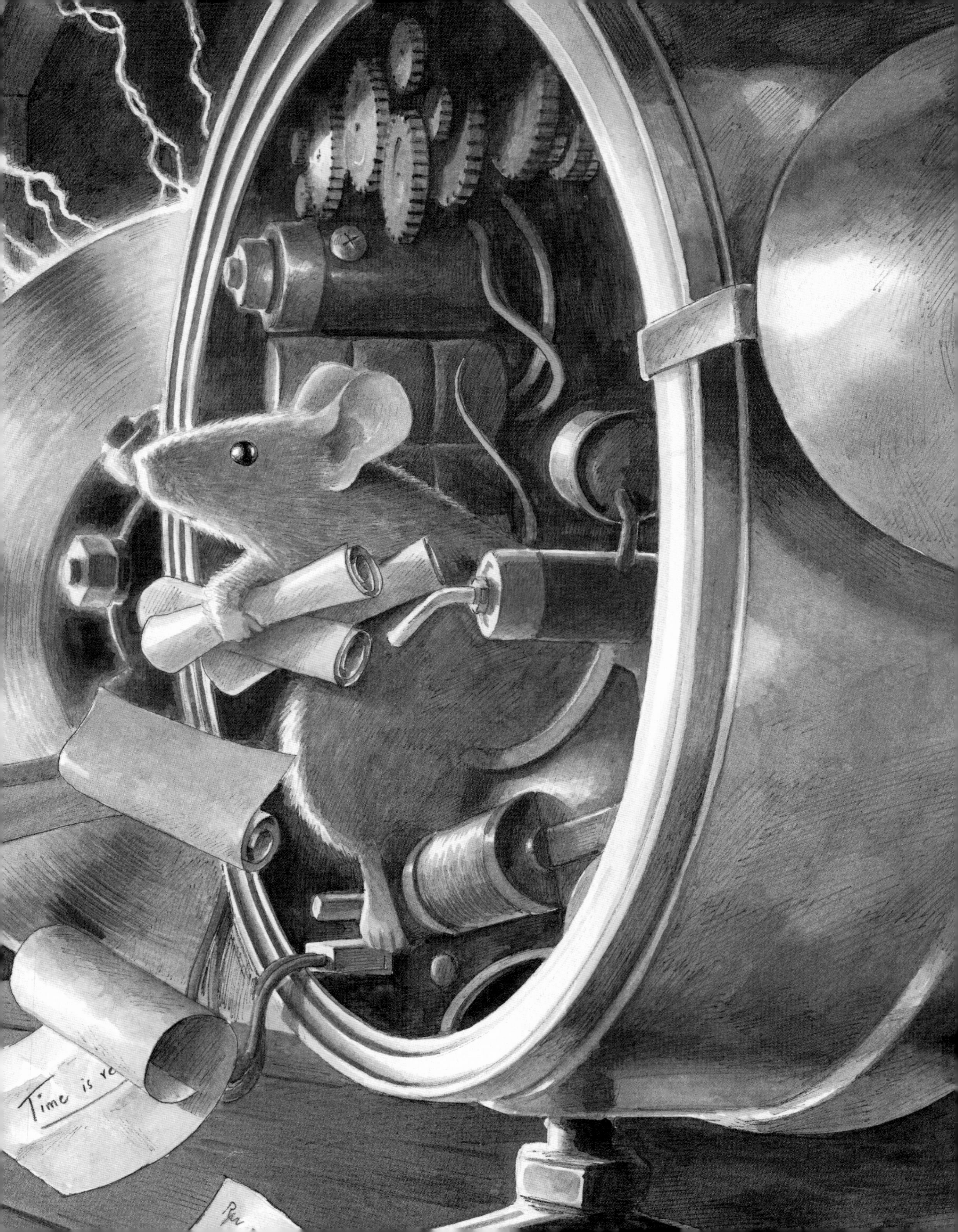
Time is re

Back through time

With a roar and a flash, mouse and time machine vanished into thin air. Albert Einstein stood incredulously in the doorway, blinded by the bright light. What had happened here? He thought he had seen something like the silhouette of a mouse in a round machine. The next moment there was nothing but a smoky patch on the floorboards surrounded by a lot of tiny footprints and a few pieces of paper floating around in the air.

When his eyes had accustomed themselves to the darkness of the attic, Einstein bent down and picked up one of the scraps of paper. When he read it, he couldn't help smiling. "I knew it."

On the piece of paper, in tiny handwriting but perfectly legible, stood just one sentence:

Time is relative.

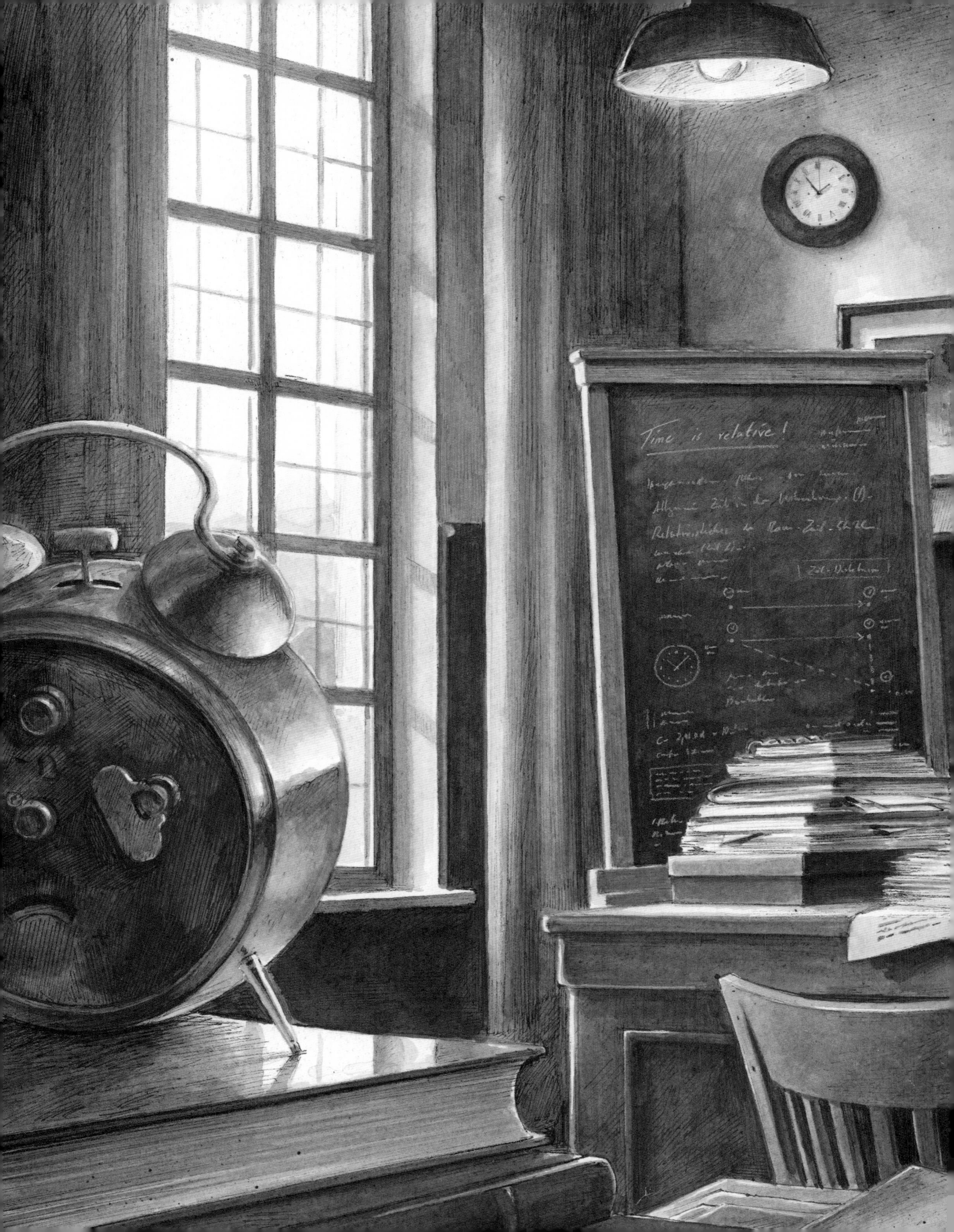
Time is relative!

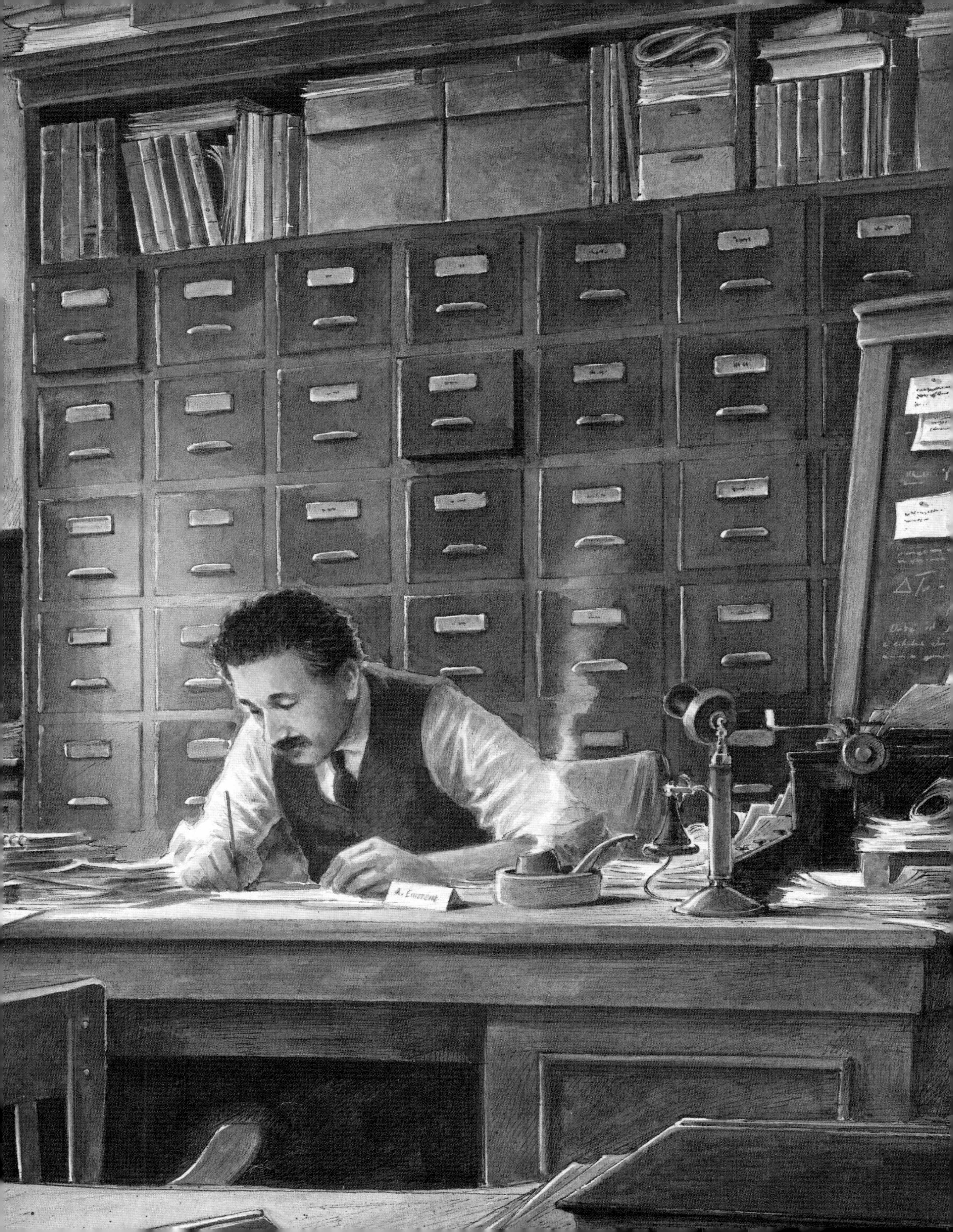
A. EINSTEIN

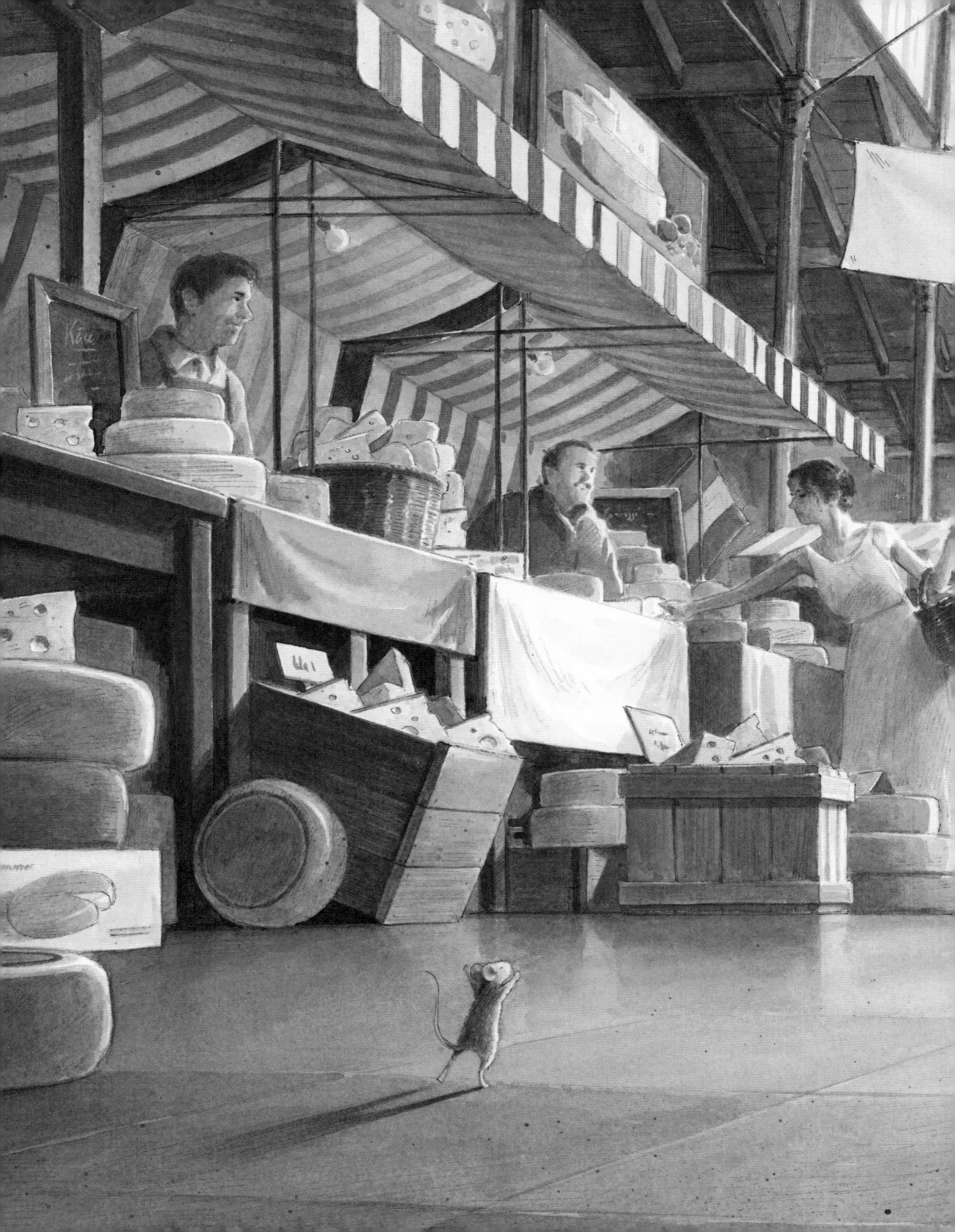
Käse

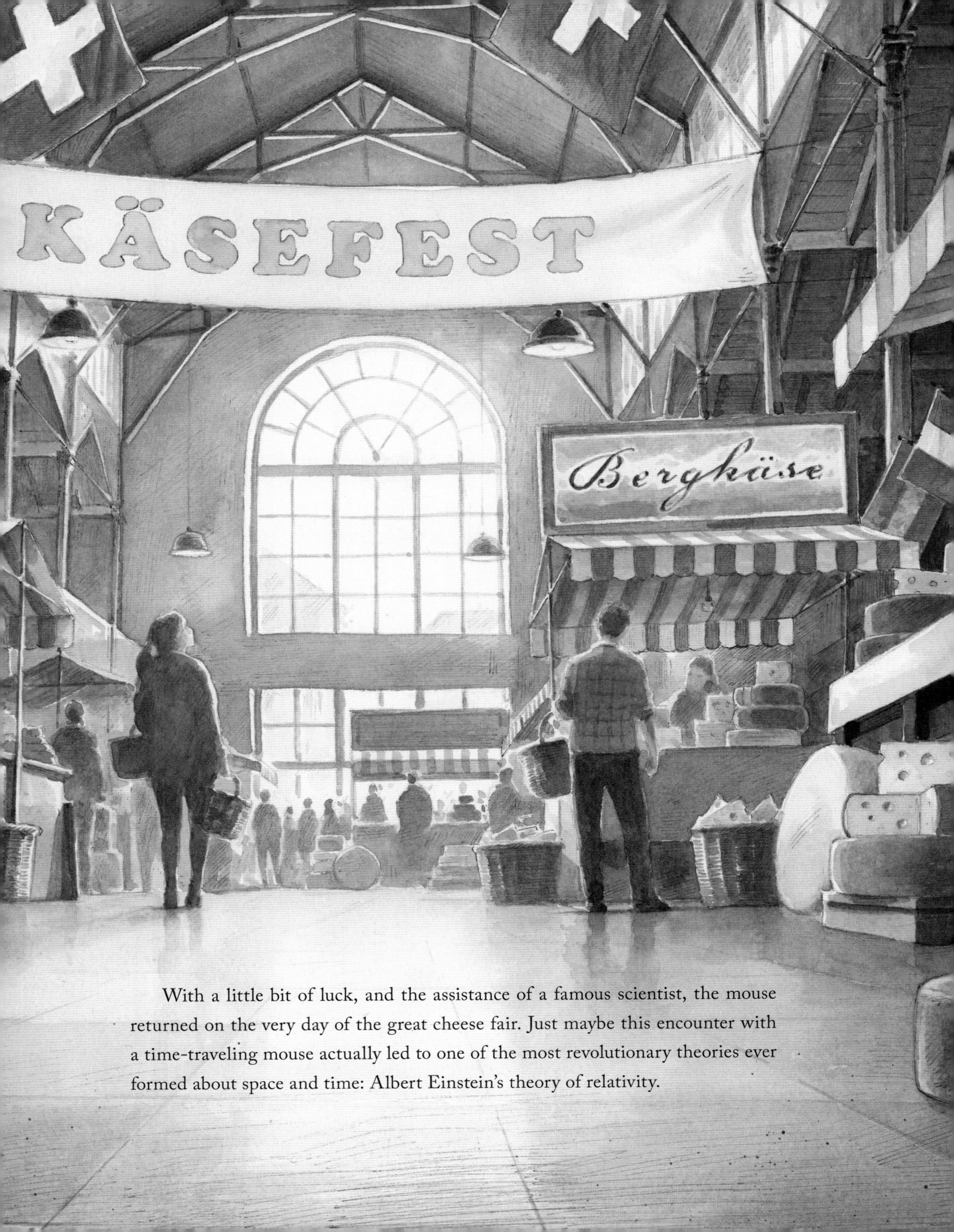
KÄSEFEST
Bergkäse

With a little bit of luck, and the assistance of a famous scientist, the mouse returned on the very day of the great cheese fair. Just maybe this encounter with a time-traveling mouse actually led to one of the most revolutionary theories ever formed about space and time: Albert Einstein's theory of relativity.

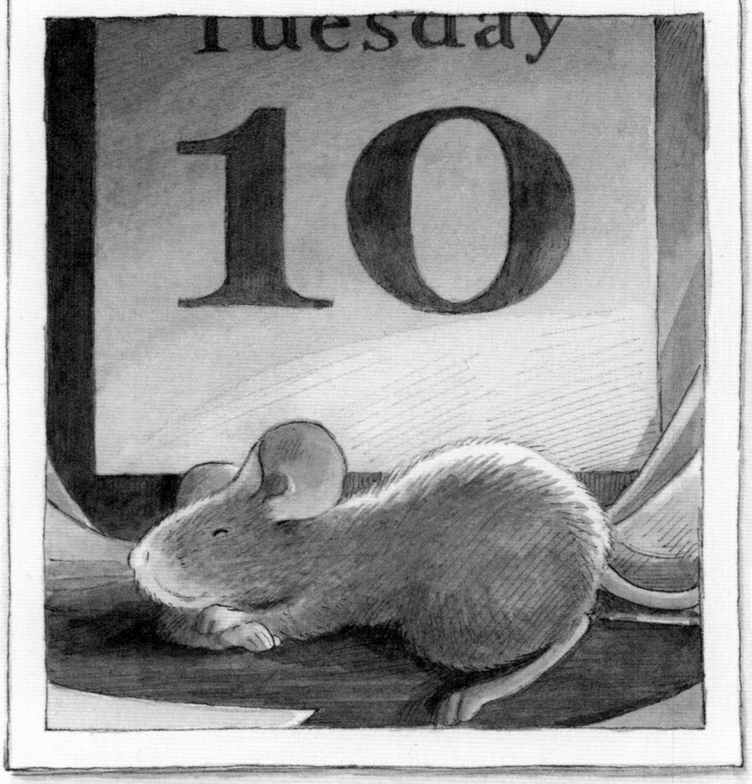
Tuesday
10

The end

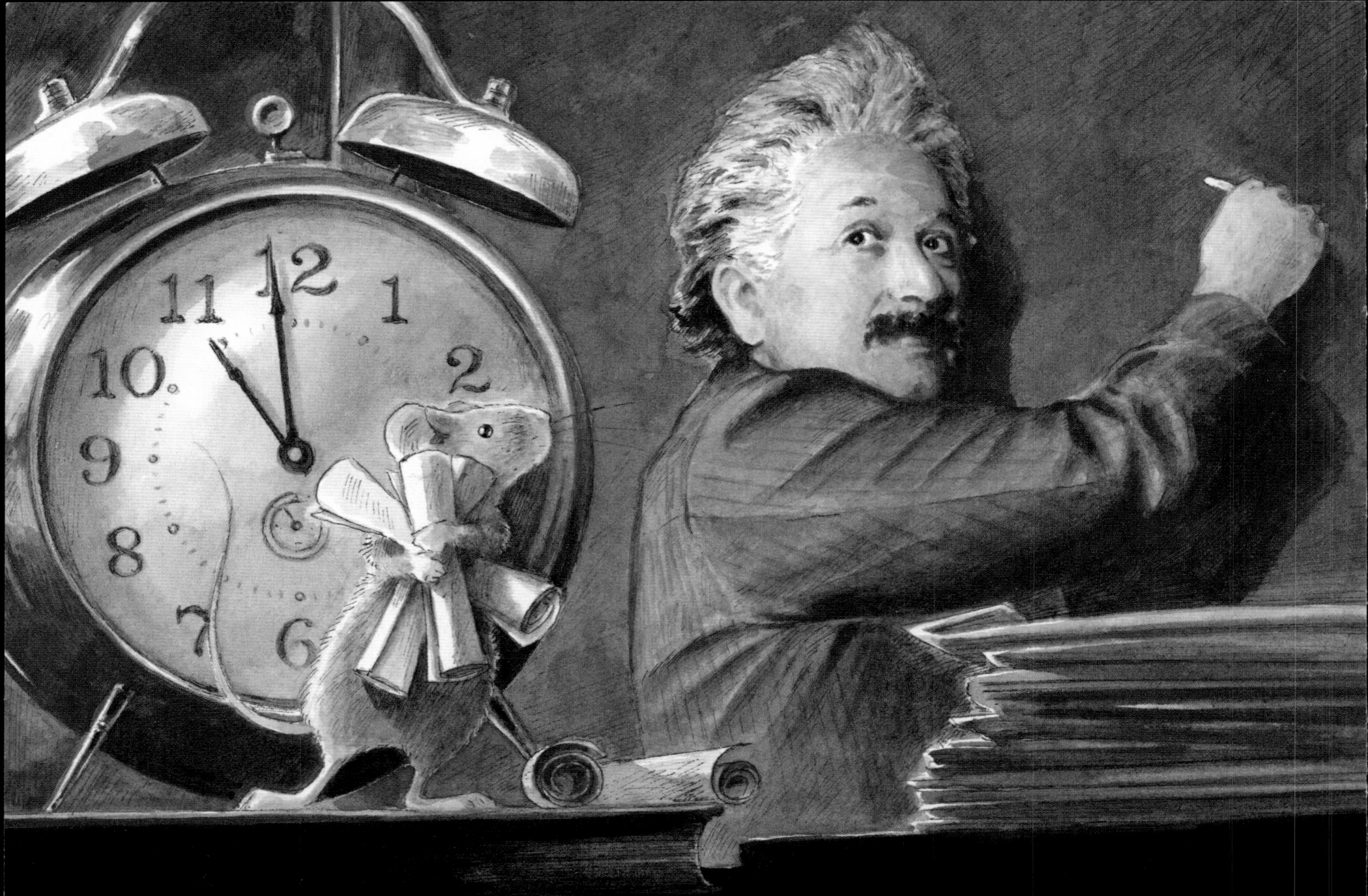

"Imagination is more important than knowledge. For knowledge is limited, whereas imagination embraces the entire world." –*Albert Einstein*

The power of imagination played an important role in Albert Einstein's work, especially in his thought experiments. In this context, the story of *Einstein—The Fantastic Journey of a Mouse Through Space and Time* plays with the idea of What would happen if? . . . In Einstein's biography, the year 1905 is known as his annus mirabilis, or miracle year. It was then that, among other things, he published his theory of special relativity and discovered the equivalence of mass and energy, which was nothing less than a new law of nature. Around the same time he was awarded his doctorate, though that was almost a secondary matter. Perhaps it was not a time-traveling mouse that was responsible for his amazing year. But whether it was or was not, it's an impressive fact than an employee of the Bernese patent office turned the world of physics on its head and completely changed our concepts of space and time.

Albert Einstein

Albert Einstein was born on March 14, 1879, in Ulm, Germany. A year later the family moved to Munich. A strange feature of his childhood is the fact that he did not learn to talk until very late. He did not finish his education but left the Munich gymnasium (high school) early, without passing any final exams, because he was not happy with the teaching methods being used there. Nevertheless, two years later he completed the Matura (Swiss equivalent of the Abitur, American equivalent of high school) at the Canton School in Aarau so that he was able to continue his studies. In 1896 he began a four-year course at the Eidgenössische Technische Hochschule, and although he got his degree, he later admitted that he regarded himself as a somewhat mediocre student. He was now qualified to teach mathematics and physics.

As he found it difficult to get a job, he followed the advice of a fellow student and applied for work at the Confederate Office for Intellectual Property in Bern. He started work there in 1902 as a "third class technical expert."

1905 is regarded as his annus mirabilis, or miracle year. In this year he published a work on the nature of electromagnetic radiation, which he thought must be composed of light quanta (also called "photons"—extremely small particles that transmit light). Next came his explanation of Brownian motion—the rapid and random movement of tiny particles then known as molecules—and an article on the electrodynamics of moving bodies. This article is better known as Einstein's theory of special relativity. In the same year he also added his description of the equivalence of mass and energy. The formula he used is probably the best known of all his gifts to humankind: $E=mc^2$.

In that same year Einstein was awarded a doctorate in physics by the University of Zürich for his work on how to determine the dimensions of molecules.

There has always been much discussion about the role played by Einstein's first wife, Mileva, who, despite the enormous difficulties for women in those days, studied the natural sciences and was herself an ambitious physicist and mathematician.

From 1908 onward Einstein taught at the University of Bern. As he was now able to earn a living from his scientific work, he resigned from the Bernese patent office in 1909. Prior to that he had been promoted to second-class technical expert.

In 1909 he was appointed Extraordinary Professor of Theoretical Physics at the University of Zürich. In 1914, he moved to Germany and lectured at the Preussische Akademie der Wissenschaften in Berlin.

Since 1909 Einstein had been working assiduously on a more general version of his theory of relativity, and he published this in November 1915 in an article entitled "The Foundation of the General Theory of Relativity."

In 1921 Einstein was awarded the Nobel Prize, although not for his General Theory of Relativity but for his work on light quanta.

As a Jew in Germany, he found himself the subject of ever-increasing hostility. Jews were now the victims of more and more persecution, injustice, and violence. Soon after Adolf Hitler and his National German Socialist Workers' Party seized power in 1933, Einstein resigned from his post at the Preussische Akademie der Wissenschaften and, like many of his Jewish colleagues, emigrated to the United States, where he found a new home in Princeton, New Jersey, and was able to continue his research at the Institute for Advanced Study.

There he devoted himself to working on the connection between his General Theory of Relativity and Quantum Theory. The correctness of both theories could be confirmed in many ways, but they could not be reconciled to each other. The search for a "Theory of Everything" has continued to this day.

Albert Einstein died on April 18, 1955, at the age of seventy-six.

Albert Einstein and Relativity

Here we shall try to offer a glimpse of the vast new world picture that Einstein describes in his special and general theories of relativity. At the heart of both theories is the concept of relativity. When something is described as "relative," it means that it depends on something else or is to be compared to something else. A simple example of this would be two trains traveling at high speed in the same direction. One train is going slightly faster than the other. For a mouse standing near the platforms and watching the trains, they would both be racing past very quickly. For another mouse sitting in the slightly slower train, however, it would seem that the faster train is only passing his own very slowly—relatively slowly—because its forward speed is *relative* to the speed at which his own train is traveling.

When something is moving, it covers a particular distance within a certain time. For instance, on the roads we might measure speeds at so many miles or kilometers per hour. Nothing moves faster than light, but even light is not infinitely fast—it travels at a particular speed. One ray moves at 186,282 miles (299,792 kilometers) per second, which is approximately three-quarters of the distance between the earth and the moon. In everyday life, of course, we never think about the *speed of light* because distances on Earth are comparatively short. When we switch on the electric light, we immediately have light. But in outer space, in spite of its astonishing speed, light still takes more than eight minutes to reach the earth from the sun. And the light from our nearest neighboring star, Alpha Centauri A, takes more than four years to reach us.

Thought experiments

The speed of light plays a very important role in Einstein's special theory of relativity. In contrast to the speed illustrated by the example of the two trains, Einstein tells us that the speed of light remains exactly the same for all observers, wherever and whenever they see it—namely, 186,282 miles per second. This can have amazing effects on time, though these are difficult to understand.

In his General Theory of Relativity, he also focuses on gravity. This is the magnetic force that holds us on the ground and also keeps our planet on its path around the sun. For example, if a mouse jumps, it will automatically fall toward the center of the earth. Only the ground stops the fall. Einstein therefore worked out the following: it makes no difference whether you are standing in an elevator on the ground or are traveling upward in another elevator in outer space at a particular speed. In both situations, you would fall out of the elevator if you weren't stopped from doing so by the floor. And if a mouse were to throw a piece of cheese up in the air, it would behave the same way in both situations: it would fall in an arc to the floor. For Einstein, the two situations are the same, or *equivalent*.

Einstein was well known for this kind of thought experiment. He would stage such examples in his mind and then draw important conclusions from what he imagined.

Einstein's time travel

For our next thought experiment, once again we need some mousy help. Here mice play the part of light, which will travel a particular distance from the left to the right side of the elevator. What is important is that for the mice the same principle applies as to the speed of light: *they have to run at the same speed in the eyes of all observers.* That is to say, they cannot appear faster or slower to anyone.

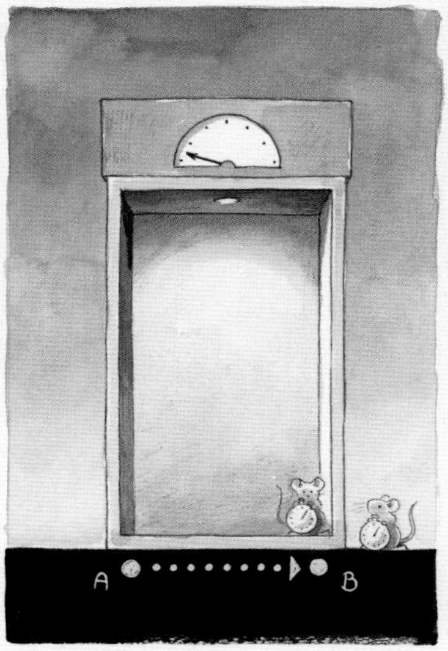
A
B

The mouse in the elevator on the ground needs five seconds to run from A to B. Meanwhile, in the elevator that is traveling through space, another mouse is also running from left to right. But at the same time, the elevator is rising upward. For an observer standing outside the elevator, this mouse has run a longer distance in the same time. A longer distance in the same time, however, means a higher speed. But isn't that impossible? *The mouse (who is playing the part of light) can only run at the same speed in the eyes of all observers.* So what has changed for the observer? Amazingly, the answer is, time. In order for the measurement of the speed to remain the same, the observer's clock must run faster than the clock inside the elevator.

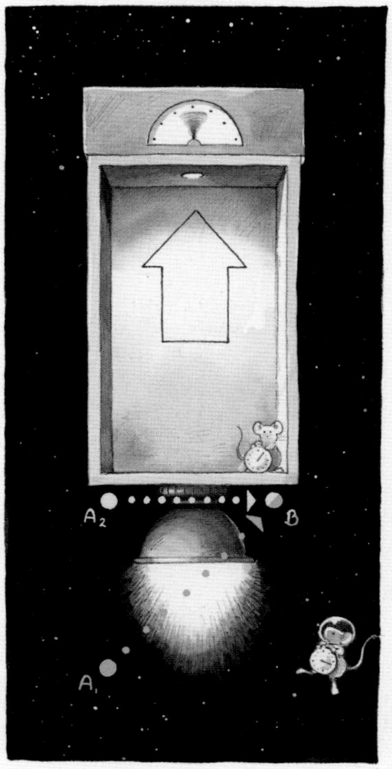
A_2
B
A_1

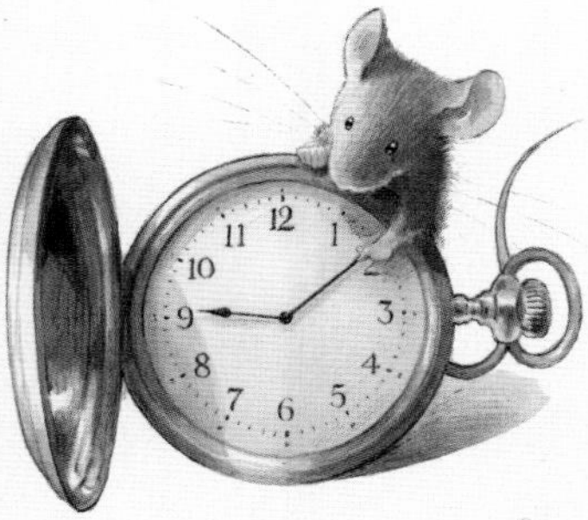

In this stretching of time lies the theoretical possibility of time travel in a spacecraft. The faster one moves away, the more slowly one's clock will tick in comparison to clocks on Earth. This stretching of time, however, only becomes apparent if one is traveling at an unimaginable and so far unachievable speed close to that of light. But if there were such a spacecraft, it would be possible to fly through space for a few days, which back on Earth would amount to several years or even decades.

A new image of space and time

For a person inside the elevator going up in space, it will seem as if everything in the universe is falling past the person. This fall even distorts the path taken by light.

Einstein concludes that in some way this must also be the case if one is simply standing on Earth. Objects, people, and mice are permanently falling toward the center of the earth, as is the universe and space. One can imagine space as a bedsheet stretched out in the air (Diagram 1).

A heavy ball will cause the sheet to bend. And likewise, heavy objects such as planets will bend space (Diagram 2).

This concept also, for the first time, explains the orbits of moons, planets, and stars. In actual fact, our moon ought to fall into the resultant spatial hollow toward the heavy object, the earth; but as the moon orbits the earth, it is fixed to a circular path. And so the "fall" in the direction of the earth is, so to speak, balanced by the centrifugal forces (a type of force that causes objects to feel pushed outward as when riding a merry-go-round) caused by the circular movement (Diagram 3).

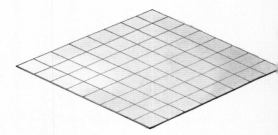

Diagram 1: Space as a two-dimensional plane

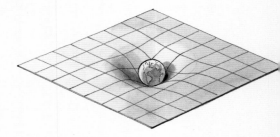

Diagram 2: A planet makes a "dent" in space

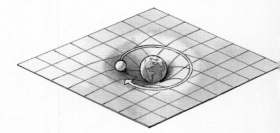

Diagram 3: The moon's orbit around the earth in curved space

The curvature of space as described in Einstein's General Theory of Relativity 1915 was a revolutionary idea. However, the proof came as early as 1919, provided by the astrophysicists Arthur Eddington and Frank Dyson. According to Einstein's predictions, the curvature of space would also cause light itself to curve. During a total eclipse of the sun, the light from the stars behind the sun could still be seen. The reason? The mass of the sun caused space to bend, and this in turn diverted the path of light.

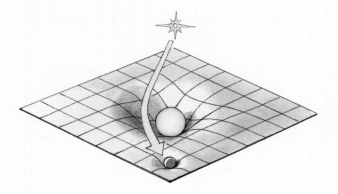

The proof of Einstein's curvature of space. Dented space deflects a ray of light. This is how in 1919 a star that was actually positioned behind the sun could be seen. The observation was only possible because the moon completely eclipsed the sun and the nearby stars became visible.

Differently ticking clocks

In Einstein's thought experiment, the clock inside the space elevator ran more slowly than those outside it. Would the same apply to clock inside the earth elevator? The answer is, yes: the curvature of space caused by heavy objects—rather like a clothesline bending under the weight of the clothes—lengthens the path taken by the light. If the speed of light is to be the same for all observers, the observers' clocks must run at different speeds. A clock at the top of a mountain will actually run slightly faster than one at sea level. During a circuit of the planet, again time will pass a fraction of a second faster than on the surface of the earth. Modern satellites and computer systems always have to balance out these unsynchronized times—another effect of relativity.

Curved space as a clothesline. When it comes close to heavy objects, such as the earth, the light's path becomes curved. The speed of light however remains constant to the observer. Therefore a watch placed at considerable distance to curved space ticks relatively faster.

This may lead to a second theoretical form of time travel. Astronauts in space travel slightly faster toward the future than people down on Earth. But this difference would not be sufficient for a perceivable journey through time. However, if the journey took place close to especially heavy high-mass cosmic objects such as quasars or black holes, the situation would be very different. In their vicinity, space is so curved that individual clocks could run considerably more slowly (or might even stop) relative to a clock on Earth.

H.G. WELLS
THE TIME MACHINE
ALBERT EINSTEIN
GENERAL THEORY OF RELATIVITY

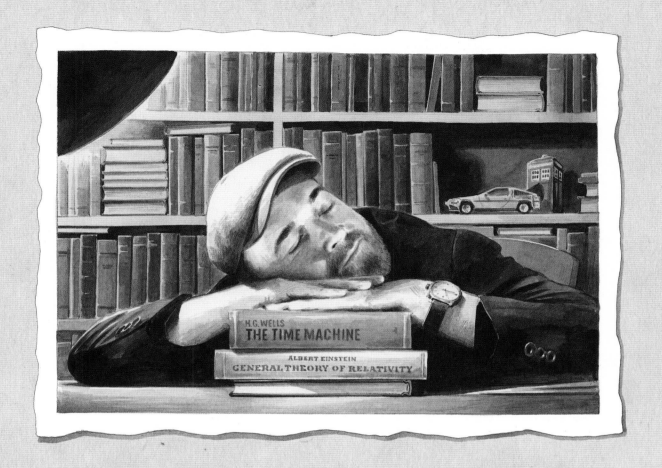

About the author

Torben Kuhlmann lives and works in Hamburg as a freelance author and illustrator of children's books. He studied illustration and communication design at the Hamburg University of Applied Sciences. He completed his studies in 2012 with the picture book *Lindbergh – The Tale of a Flying Mouse,* which was published shortly afterward by NordSüd Verlag. This soon became a best seller, as did the mouse adventures of *Armstrong – The Adventurous Journey of a Mouse to the Moon* and *Edison – The Mystery of the Missing Mouse Treasure.* This trilogy of books has been translated into more than thirty different languages. The latest adventure, *Einstein – The Fantastic Journey of a Mouse Through Space and Time* – again superbly illustrated in watercolors and pencil – takes the series into the realms of science fiction, inspired by the example of the great authors who have written in this genre.

5¢
LINDBERGH
ARMSTRONG
10¢
EDISON
25¢

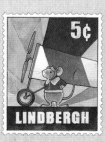

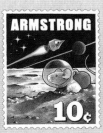

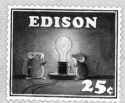

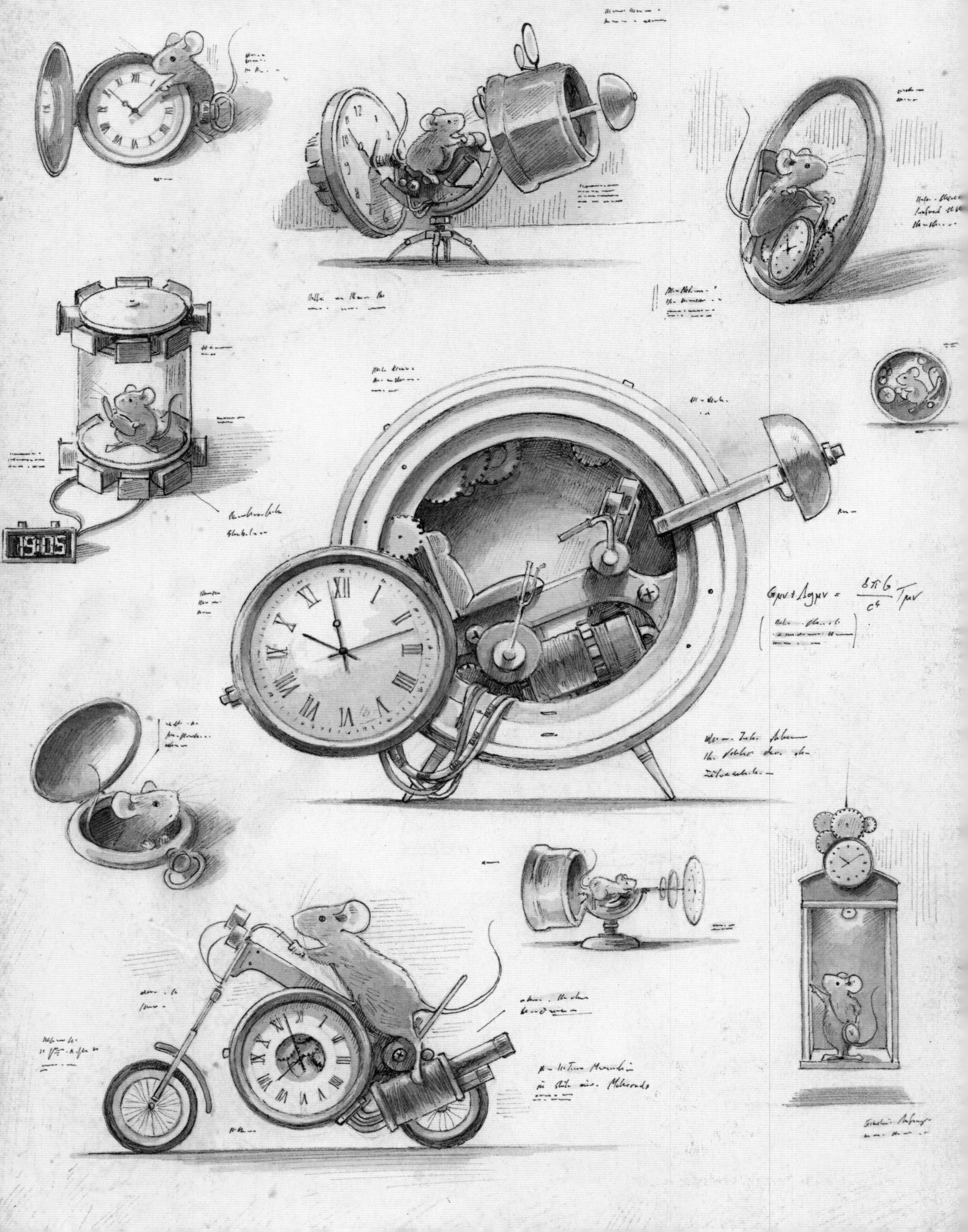
19:05
Gμν + Λgμν = 8πG/c⁴ Tμν